SEAL

MISSION #1

STORY
SEA SNIPERS®

WRITER
RICH HUNSINGER

ARTISTS
RICH HUNSINGER
SEA SNIPERS®

EDITORS
SEA SNIPERS®

THE SEA SNIPERS® ARE:

RATOR, SNAKEBITE, SPORTOFU, SHOOTER, WALLY, KOKIDO, TUEFEL HUNDEN, SKINMAN, SHOWSTOPER, HOBO, TWIST, GRIFTER, RAIDEN, BREACH

WITH APPEARANCES BY:

DREW SINDERS, JESSICA SINDERS, KATE HUNSINGER, ANDRES VALDES, VINCE SURIANI, CHARLIE BARNES, RICHARD HUNSINGER

SPECIAL THANKS:

KATE HUNSINGER, AUNT SUSAN, MOMS CRISPY RIBS, THE PITTMAN BOYS, SOCOM 2, PHIL PERRY, COTTON, PATTY, SAGE, MATTHEW, ELLA, STACEY, JENNIFER, JILLIAN, REECE, 33 BKY, JENNIFER CANALE, THOMAS AND MARY CANALE, AL AND BEV EVANS, TOSCHE, MICHELLE AND MIA MCCARTHY, SMOKED OLD FASHIONEDS, THE GREAT OUTDOORS, CHRISTINA, AUGUST, NATHAN, BROOKE, LIAM, THE CARROLLS, DARREN GARDNER AKA ORAKIX

SEAL™ UNIVERSE CREATED BY THE SEA SNIPERS®
BUSINESS INQUIRIES: WWW.SEASNIPERS.NET

© 2022 COPYRIGHT COMBAT DEVELOPMENT LLC. ALL RIGHTS RESERVED. THIS IS A WORK OF FICTION. ANY DEPICTIONS OF PERSONS, NAMES, AND/OR ORGANIZATIONS LIVING OR DEAD ARE FOR ENTERTAINMENT PURPOSES ONLY AND SHOULD NOT BE TAKEN LITERALLY. ALL ENTITIES, PEOPLE AND ORGANIZATIONS IN THIS BOOK ARE PLAYING A ROLE IN THE FICTIONAL SEAL™ UNIVERSE.

INTRODUCTION

AFTER YEARS OF HARD WORK, THE SEA SNIPERS® ARE PROUD TO PRESENT THE FIRST ISSUE OF SEAL™.

OUR STORY FOLLOWS A TEAM OF RETIRED NAVY SEALS CALLED BACK TO ACTIVE DUTY TO COMBAT LONE-WOLF TERRORISM ON AMERICAN SOIL.

WITH MISSIONS TAKING PLACE ALL OVER NORTH AMERICA, THIS IS THE FIRST TIME IN HISTORY THAT SEALS WILL BE DEPLOYED TO PROTECT THE U.S. AND ITS BORDERS.

JOIN SEAL TEAM 55 AS THEY GET BACK TO WORK AND LEARN OF ONE OF THE BIGGEST THREATS THE WORLD HAS EVER SEEN, AND UNRAVEL THE MYSTERY OF THE "LONE WOLVES" THAT ARE ASSAULTING AMERICA.

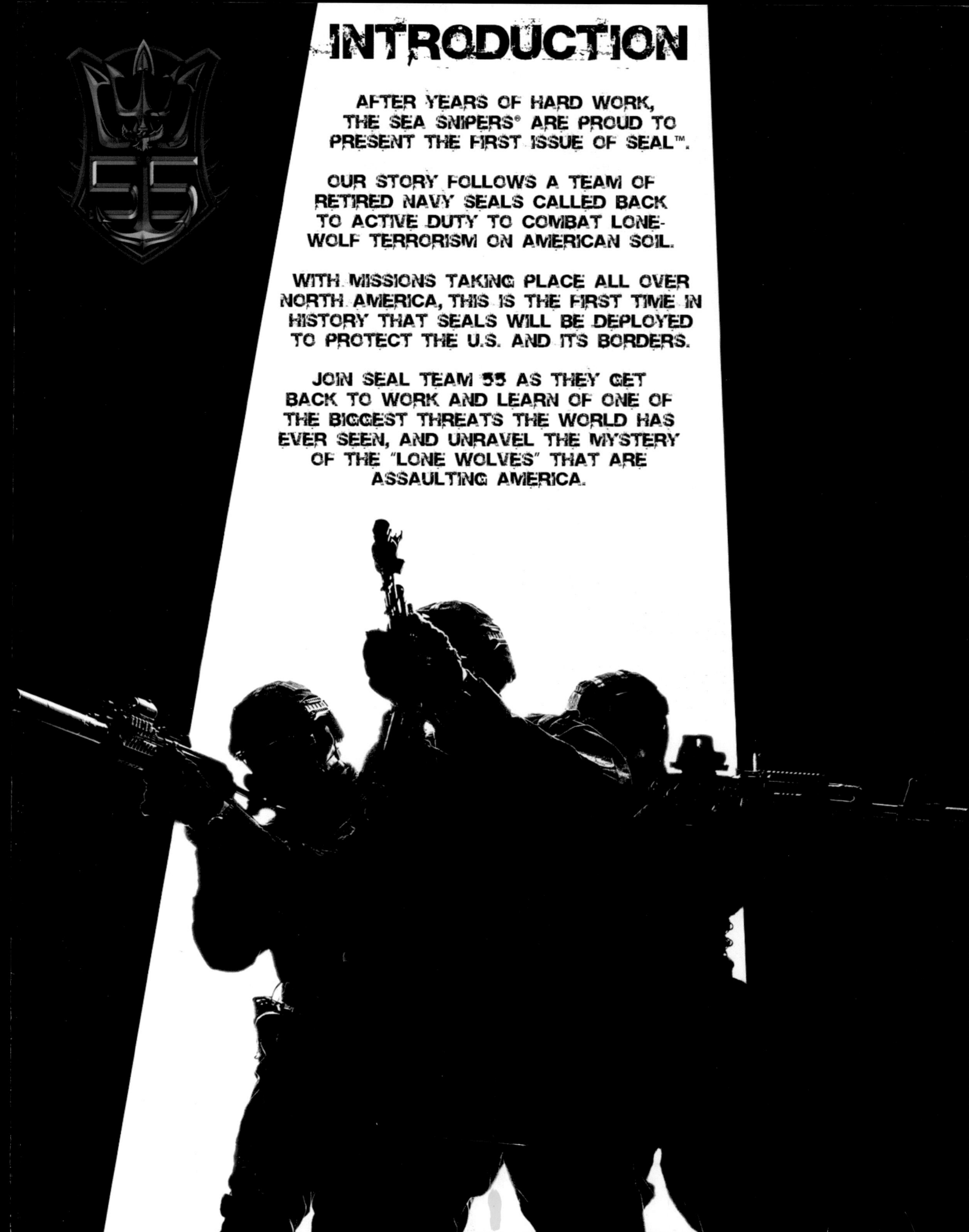

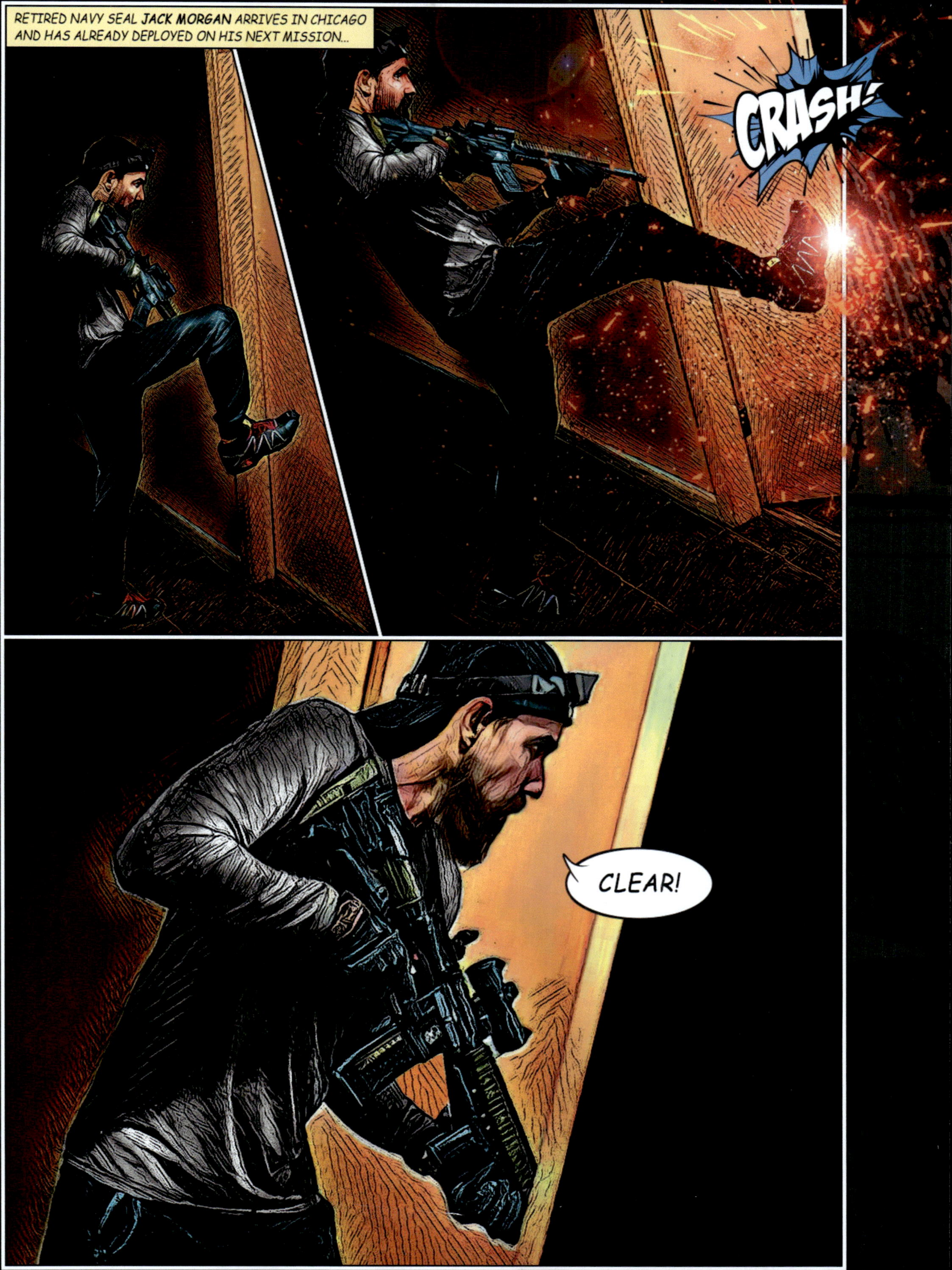
RETIRED NAVY SEAL JACK MORGAN ARRIVES IN CHICAGO AND HAS ALREADY DEPLOYED ON HIS NEXT MISSION...
CRASH!
CLEAR!

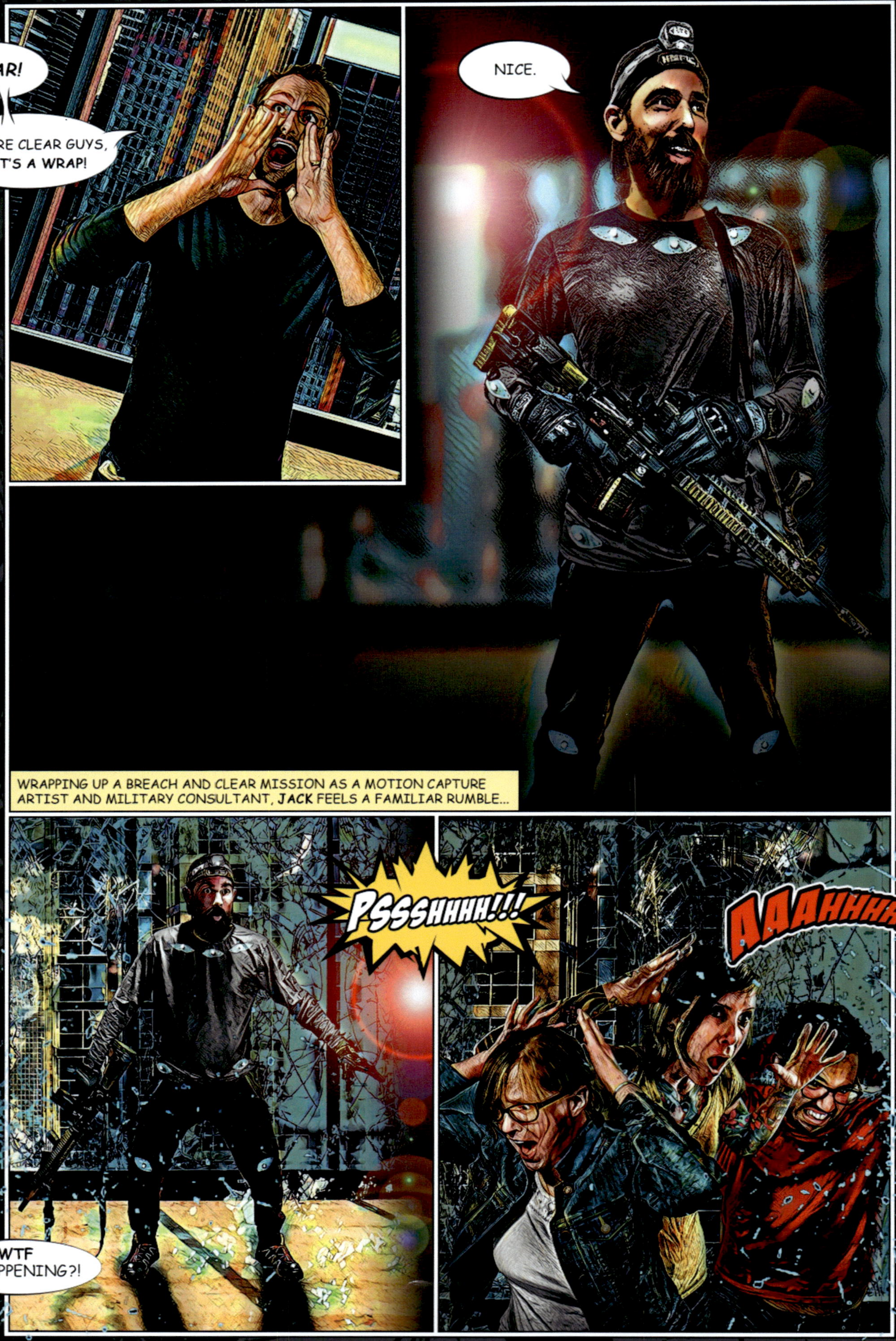
CLEAR!
OK WE'RE CLEAR GUYS, THAT'S A WRAP!
NICE.
WRAPPING UP A BREACH AND CLEAR MISSION AS A MOTION CAPTURE ARTIST AND MILITARY CONSULTANT, JACK FEELS A FAMILIAR RUMBLE...
PSSSHHHH!!!
WTF IS HAPPENING?!
AAAHHHH!!!

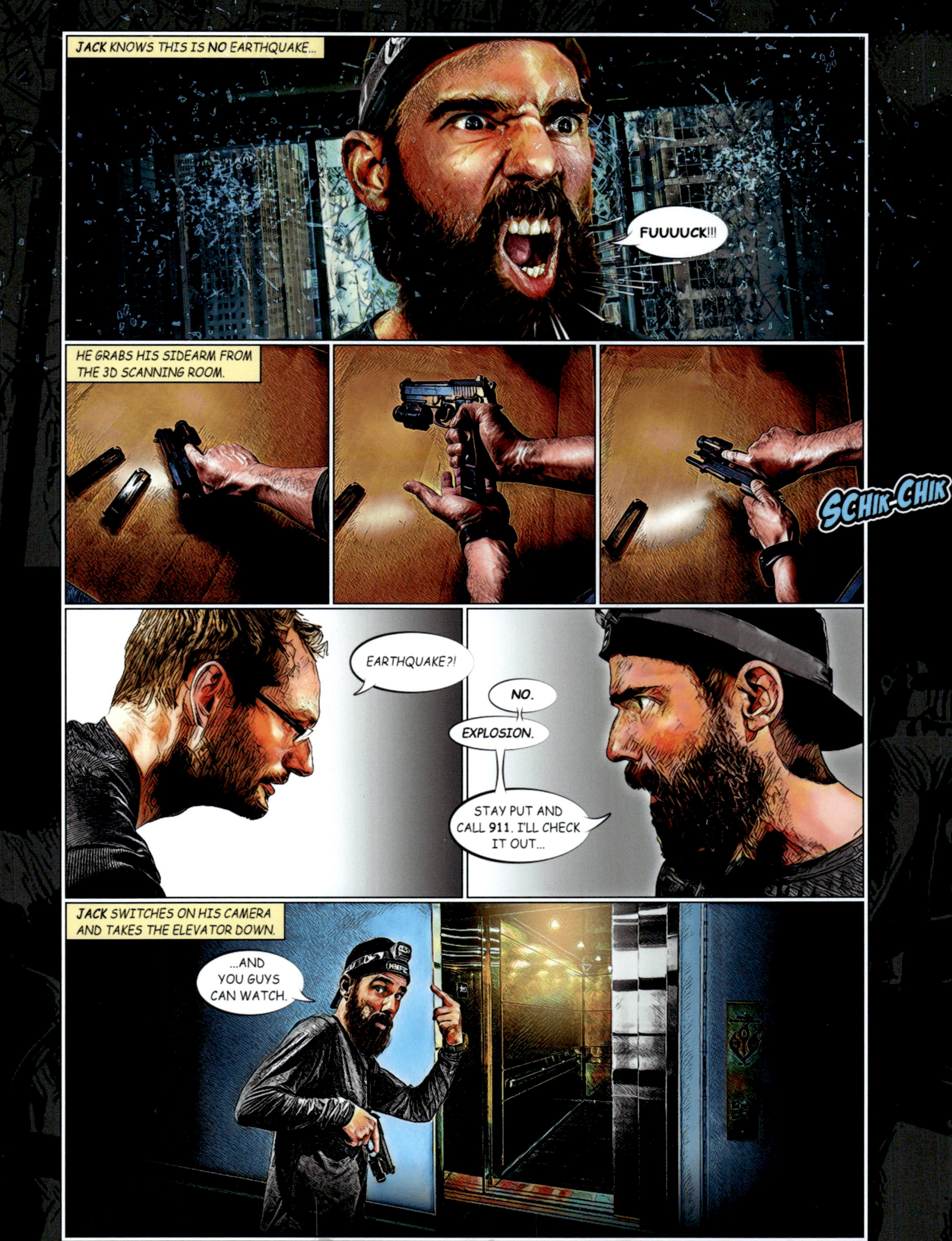
JACK KNOWS THIS IS NO EARTHQUAKE...
FUUUUCK!!!
HE GRABS HIS SIDEARM FROM THE 3D SCANNING ROOM.
SCHIK-CHIK
EARTHQUAKE?!
NO.
EXPLOSION.
STAY PUT AND CALL 911. I'LL CHECK IT OUT...
JACK SWITCHES ON HIS CAMERA AND TAKES THE ELEVATOR DOWN.
...AND YOU GUYS CAN WATCH.

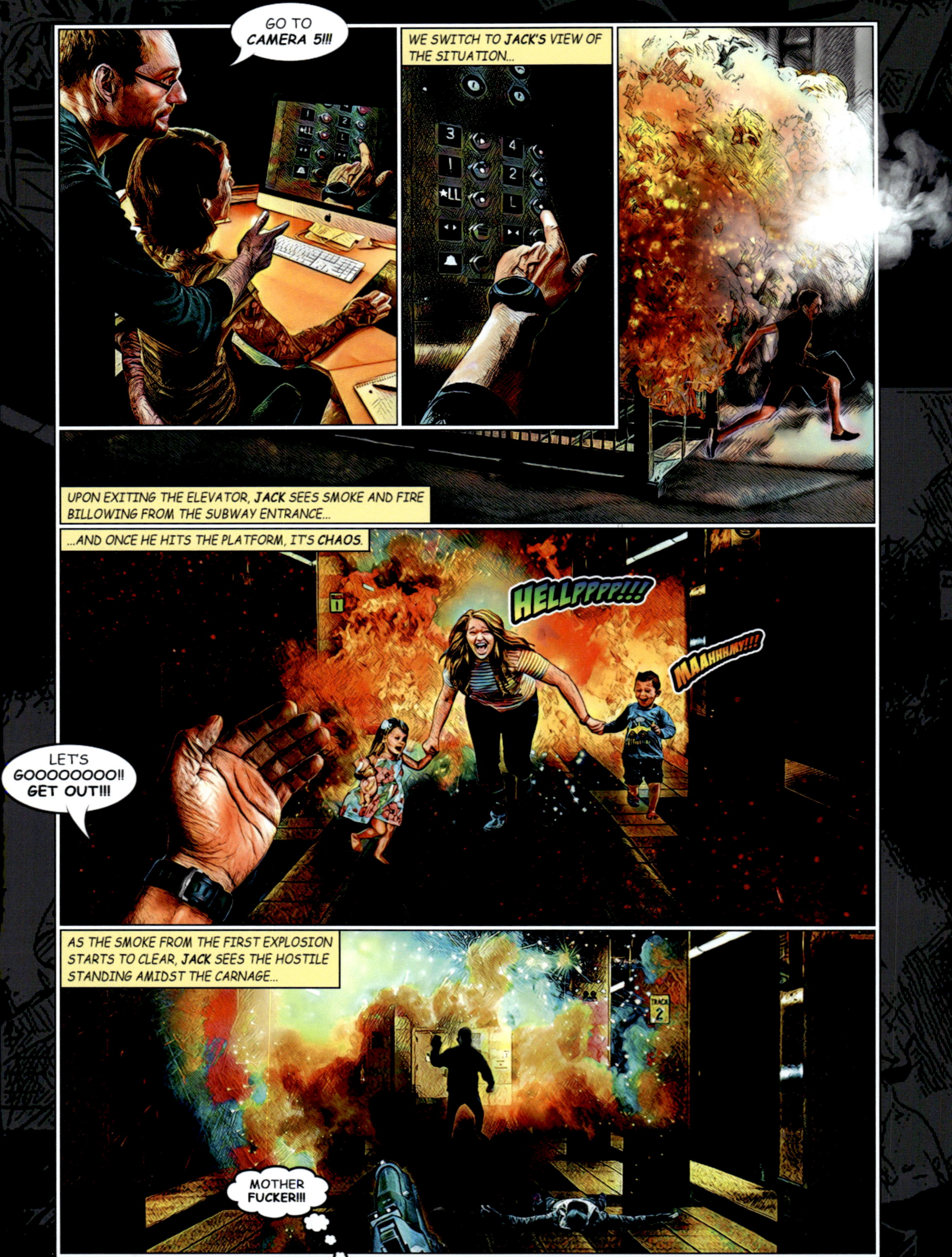
GO TO CAMERA 5!!!
WE SWITCH TO JACK'S VIEW OF THE SITUATION...
UPON EXITING THE ELEVATOR, JACK SEES SMOKE AND FIRE BILLOWING FROM THE SUBWAY ENTRANCE...
...AND ONCE HE HITS THE PLATFORM, IT'S CHAOS.
HELLPPPP!!!
MAAHHHMY!!!
LET'S GOOOOOOOO!! GET OUT!!!
AS THE SMOKE FROM THE FIRST EXPLOSION STARTS TO CLEAR, JACK SEES THE HOSTILE STANDING AMIDST THE CARNAGE...
MOTHER FUCKER!!!

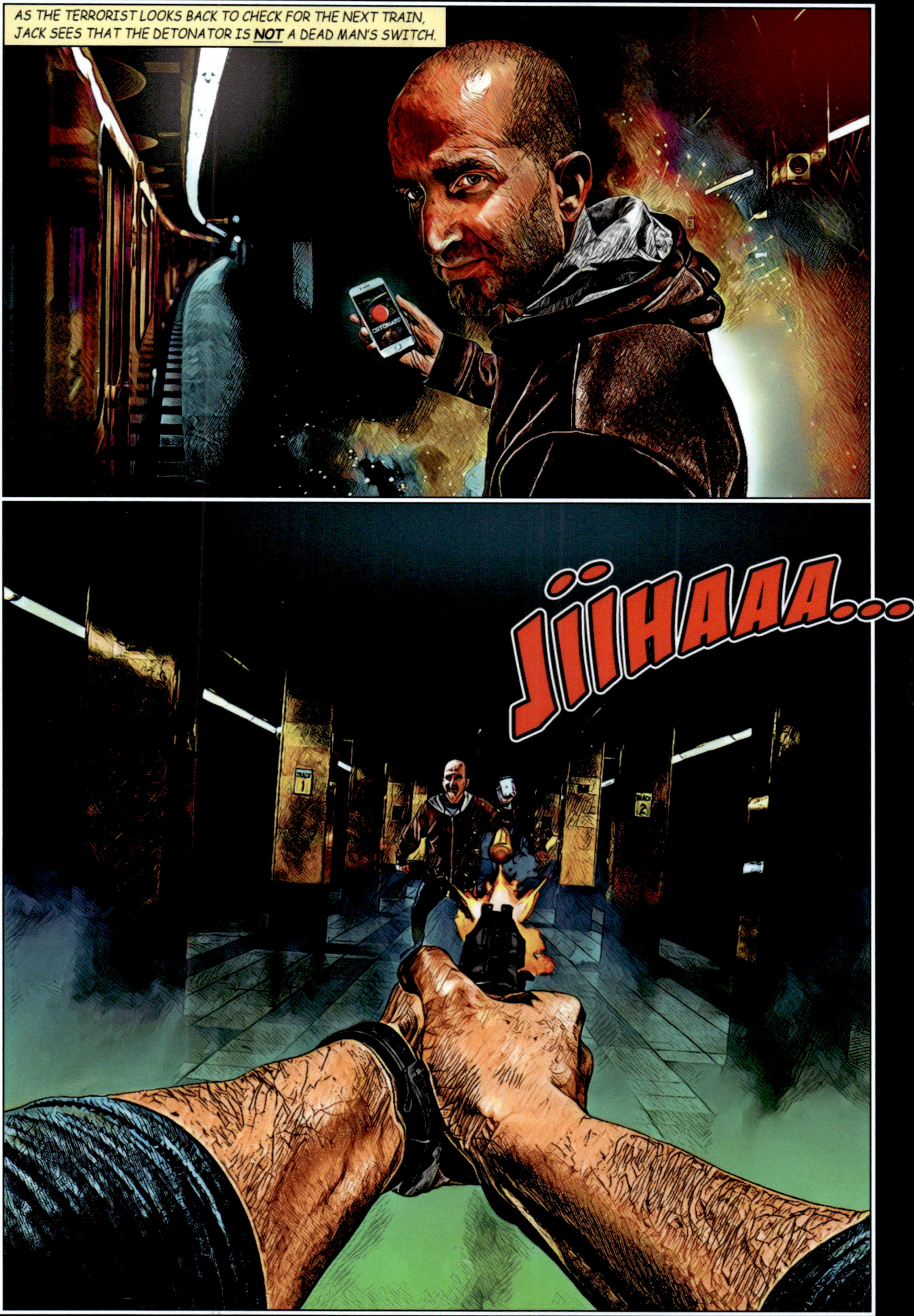
AS THE TERRORIST LOOKS BACK TO CHECK FOR THE NEXT TRAIN, JACK SEES THAT THE DETONATOR IS **NOT** A DEAD MAN'S SWITCH.
JIIHAAA...

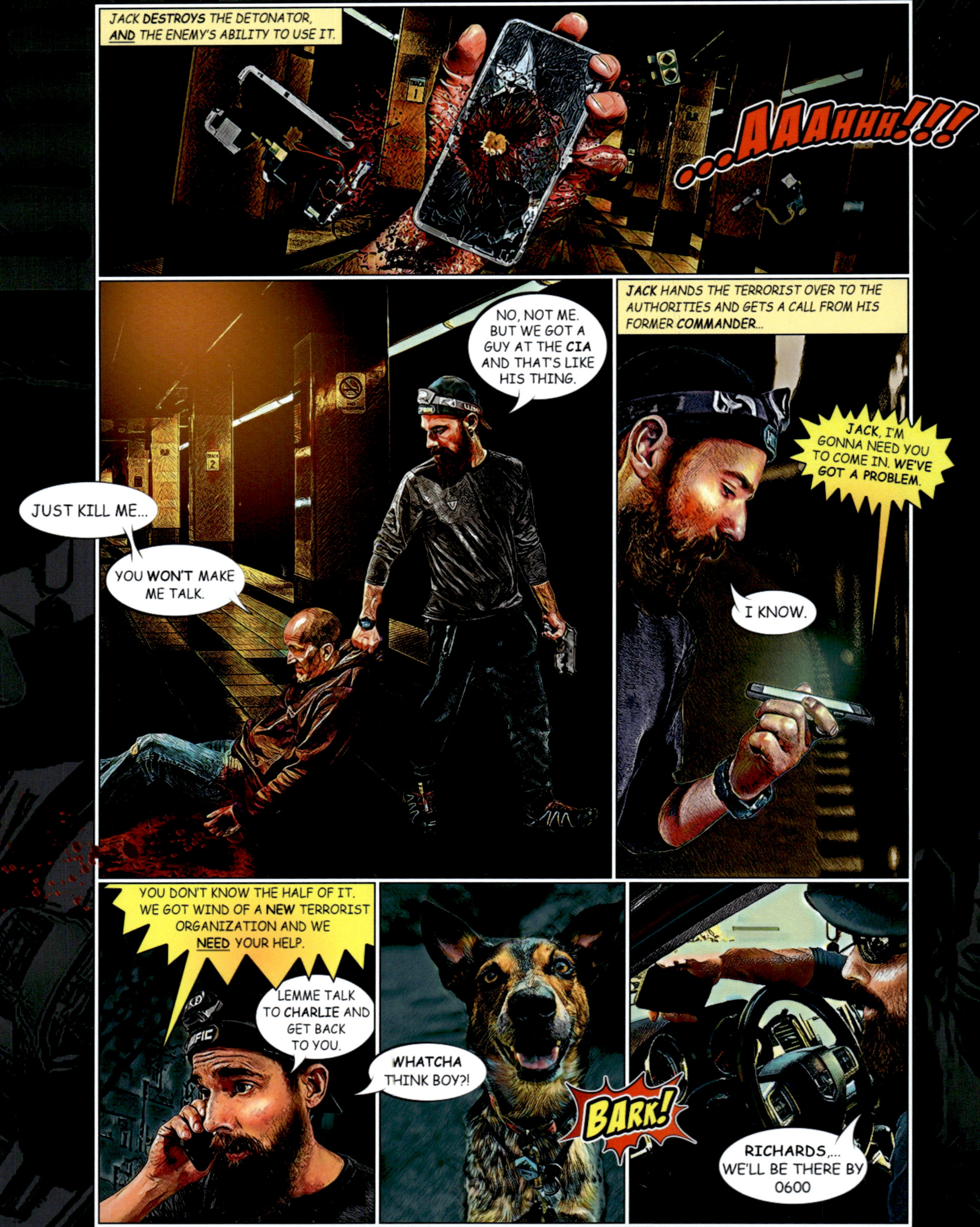

JACK DESTROYS THE DETONATOR, AND THE ENEMY'S ABILITY TO USE IT.
...AAAHHH!!!
NO, NOT ME. BUT WE GOT A GUY AT THE CIA AND THAT'S LIKE HIS THING.
JUST KILL ME...
YOU WON'T MAKE ME TALK.
JACK HANDS THE TERRORIST OVER TO THE AUTHORITIES AND GETS A CALL FROM HIS FORMER COMMANDER...
JACK, I'M GONNA NEED YOU TO COME IN. WE'VE GOT A PROBLEM.
I KNOW.
YOU DON'T KNOW THE HALF OF IT. WE GOT WIND OF A NEW TERRORIST ORGANIZATION AND WE NEED YOUR HELP.
LEMME TALK TO CHARLIE AND GET BACK TO YOU.
WHATCHA THINK BOY?!
BARK!
RICHARDS,... WE'LL BE THERE BY 0600

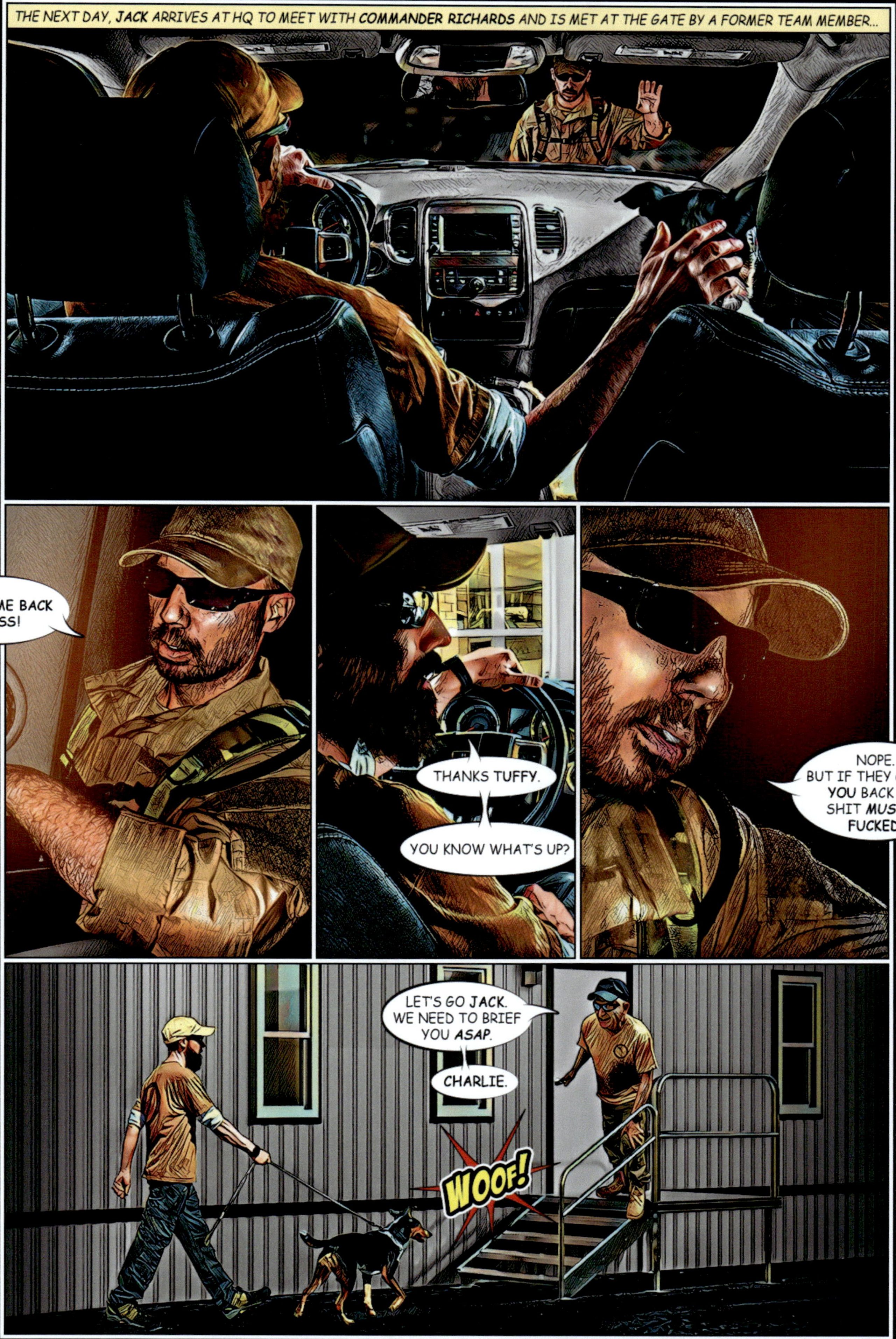
THE NEXT DAY, JACK ARRIVES AT HQ TO MEET WITH COMMANDER RICHARDS AND IS MET AT THE GATE BY A FORMER TEAM MEMBER...
WELCOME BACK BOSS!
THANKS TUFFY.
YOU KNOW WHAT'S UP?
NOPE. BUT IF THEY CALLED YOU BACK IN, SHIT MUST BE FUCKED.
LET'S GO JACK. WE NEED TO BRIEF YOU ASAP.
CHARLIE.
WOOF!

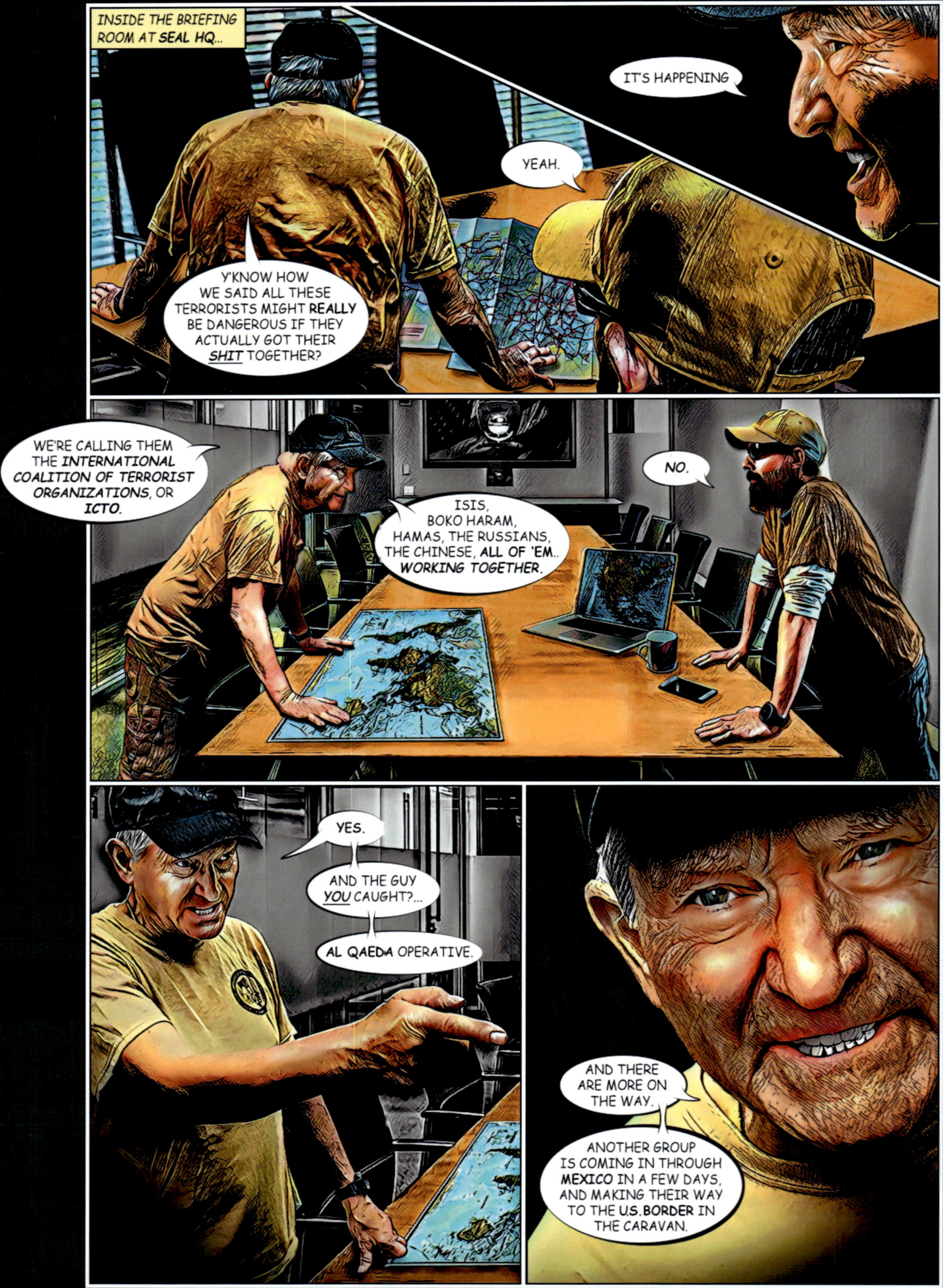
INSIDE THE BRIEFING ROOM AT SEAL HQ...
IT'S HAPPENING
YEAH.
Y'KNOW HOW WE SAID ALL THESE TERRORISTS MIGHT REALLY BE DANGEROUS IF THEY ACTUALLY GOT THEIR SHIT TOGETHER?
WE'RE CALLING THEM THE INTERNATIONAL COALITION OF TERRORIST ORGANIZATIONS, OR ICTO.
NO.
ISIS, BOKO HARAM, HAMAS, THE RUSSIANS, THE CHINESE, ALL OF 'EM.. WORKING TOGETHER.
YES.
AND THE GUY YOU CAUGHT?...
AL QAEDA OPERATIVE.
AND THERE ARE MORE ON THE WAY.
ANOTHER GROUP IS COMING IN THROUGH MEXICO IN A FEW DAYS, AND MAKING THEIR WAY TO THE U.S. BORDER IN THE CARAVAN.

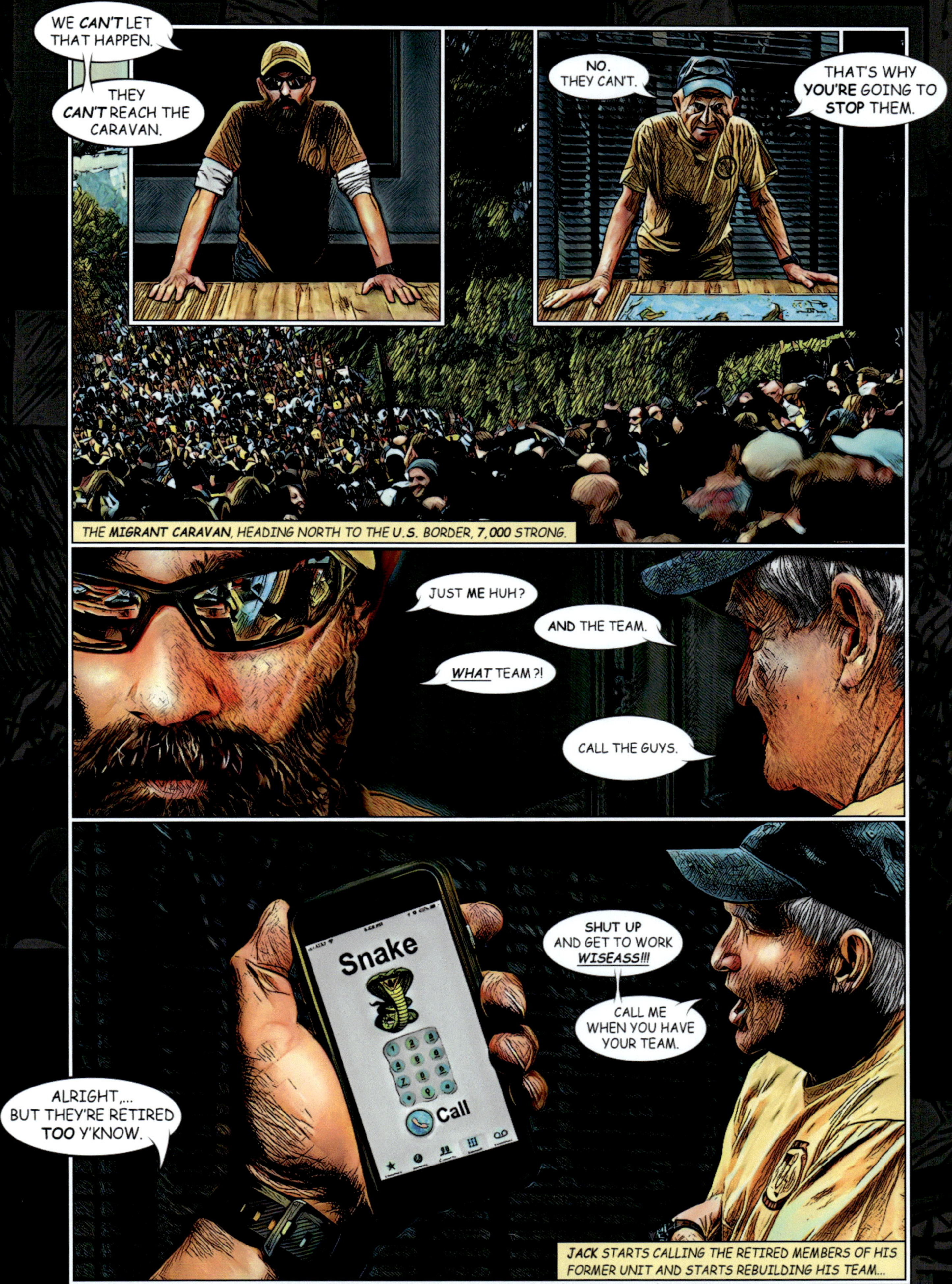
WE CAN'T LET THAT HAPPEN.
THEY CAN'T REACH THE CARAVAN.
NO. THEY CAN'T.
THAT'S WHY YOU'RE GOING TO STOP THEM.
THE MIGRANT CARAVAN, HEADING NORTH TO THE U.S. BORDER, 7,000 STRONG.
JUST ME HUH?
AND THE TEAM.
WHAT TEAM ?!
CALL THE GUYS.
Snake
Call
SHUT UP AND GET TO WORK WISEASS!!!
CALL ME WHEN YOU HAVE YOUR TEAM.
ALRIGHT,... BUT THEY'RE RETIRED TOO Y'KNOW.
JACK STARTS CALLING THE RETIRED MEMBERS OF HIS FORMER UNIT AND STARTS REBUILDING HIS TEAM...

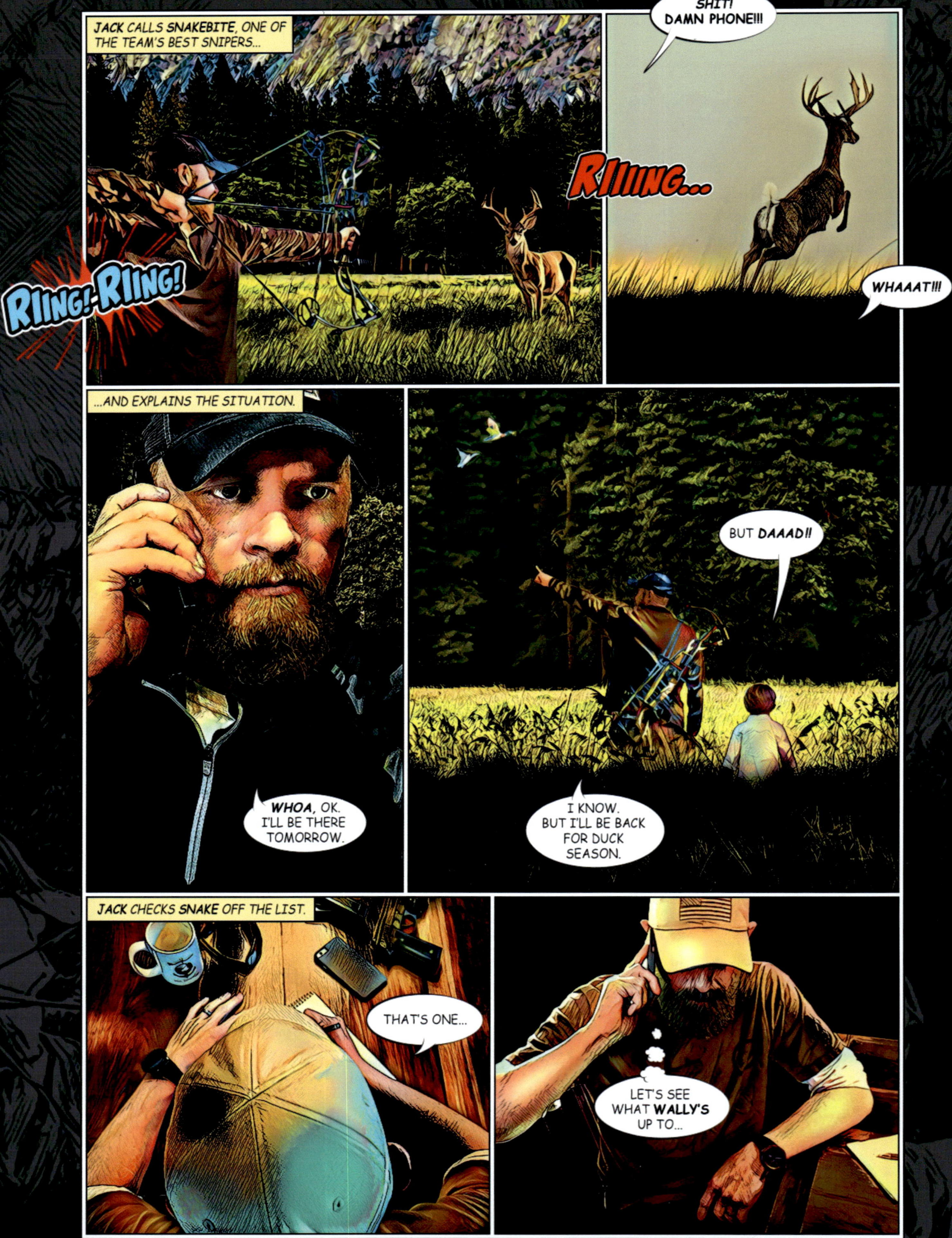

JACK CALLS SNAKEBITE, ONE OF THE TEAM'S BEST SNIPERS...
RIING! RIING!
RIIIING...
SHIT! DAMN PHONE!!!
WHAAAT!!!
...AND EXPLAINS THE SITUATION.
WHOA, OK. I'LL BE THERE TOMORROW.
BUT DAAAD!!
I KNOW. BUT I'LL BE BACK FOR DUCK SEASON.
JACK CHECKS SNAKE OFF THE LIST.
THAT'S ONE...
LET'S SEE WHAT WALLY'S UP TO...

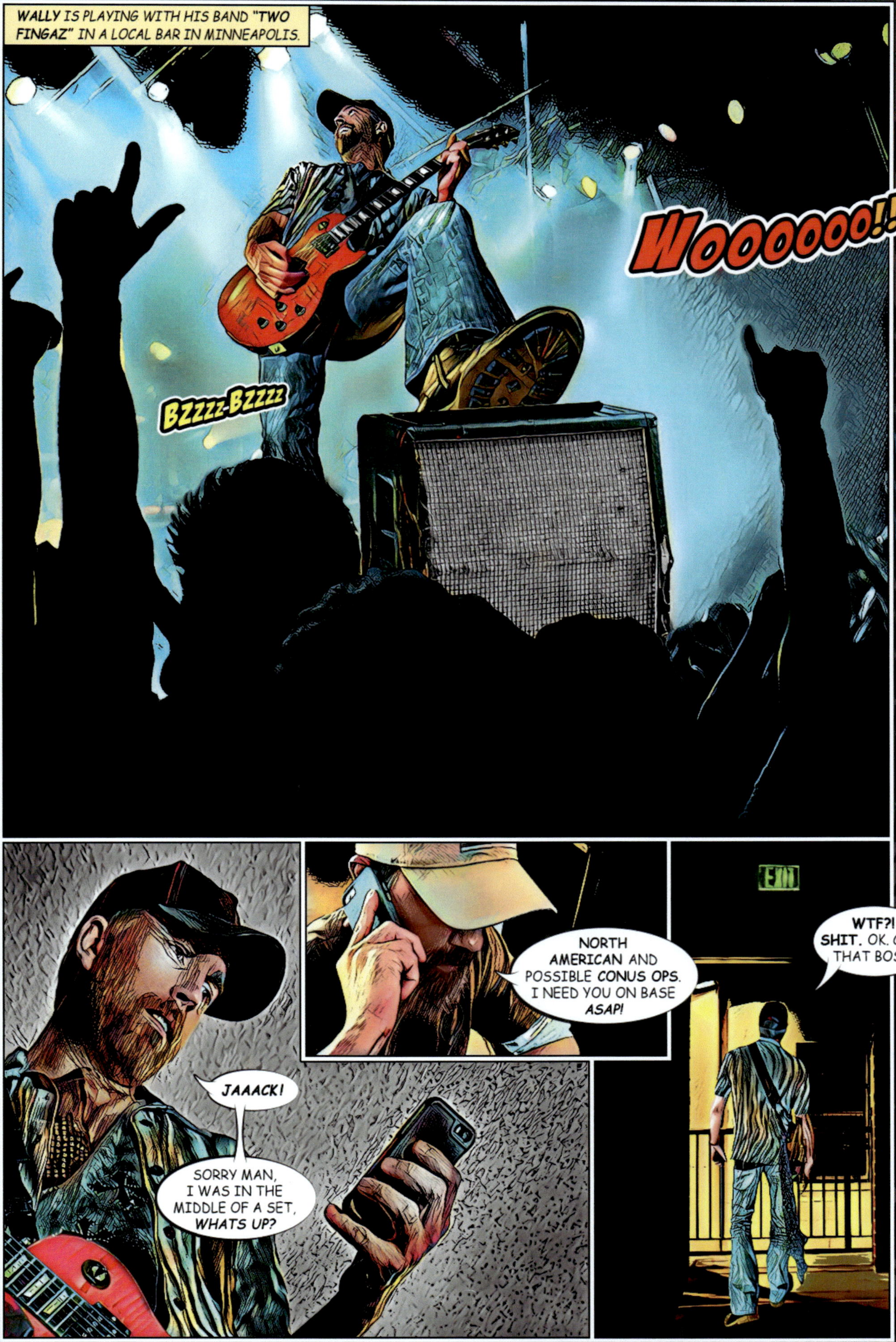
WALLY IS PLAYING WITH HIS BAND "TWO FINGAZ" IN A LOCAL BAR IN MINNEAPOLIS.
WOOOOOO!!!
BZZZZ-BZZZZ
JAAACK!
SORRY MAN, I WAS IN THE MIDDLE OF A SET, WHATS UP?
NORTH AMERICAN AND POSSIBLE CONUS OPS. I NEED YOU ON BASE ASAP!
WTF?! SHIT. OK. COPY THAT BOSS.

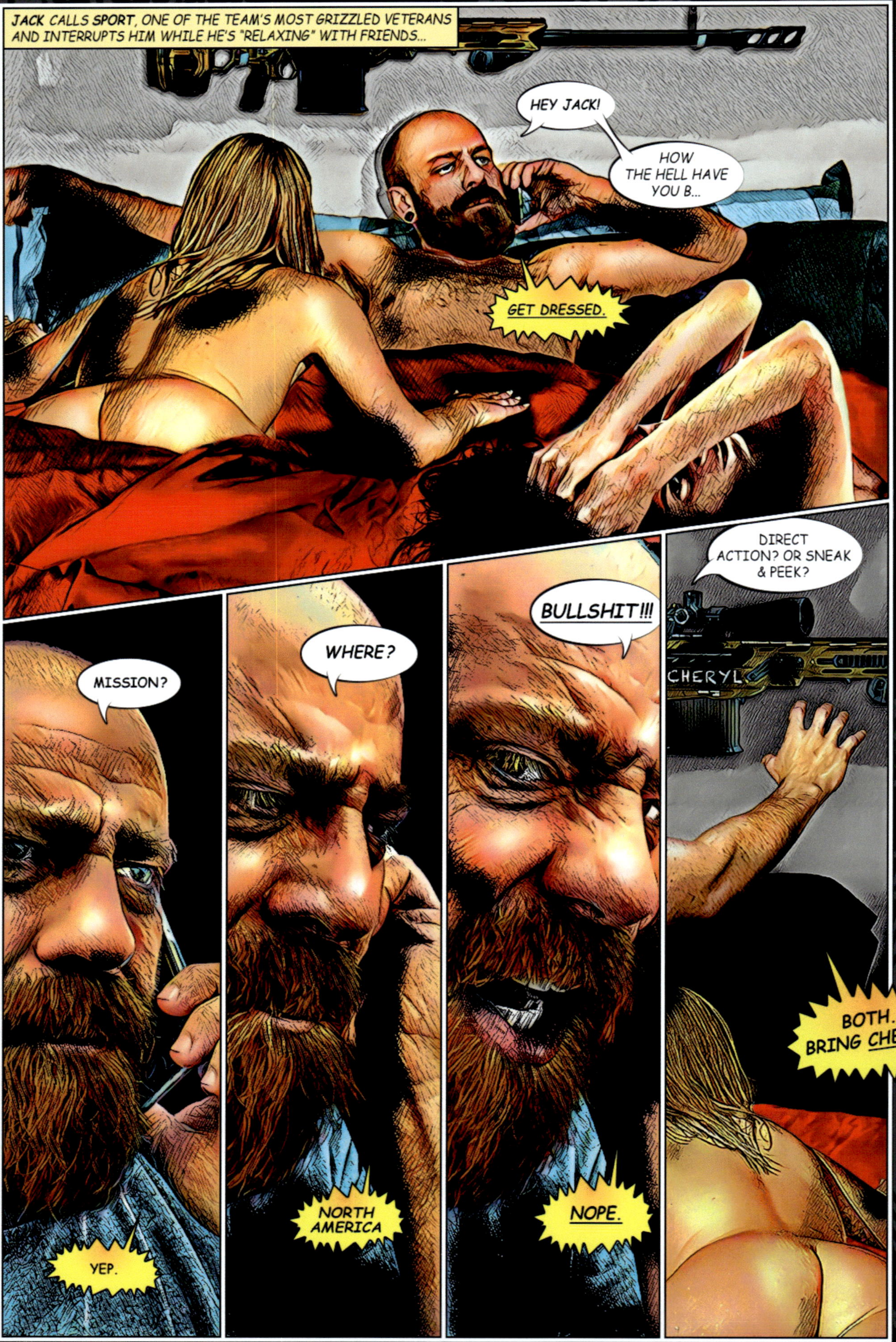
JACK CALLS SPORT, ONE OF THE TEAM'S MOST GRIZZLED VETERANS AND INTERRUPTS HIM WHILE HE'S "RELAXING" WITH FRIENDS...
HEY JACK!
HOW THE HELL HAVE YOU B...
GET DRESSED.
MISSION?
YEP.
WHERE?
NORTH AMERICA
BULLSHIT!!!
NOPE.
DIRECT ACTION? OR SNEAK & PEEK?
CHERYL
BOTH. BRING CHERYL.

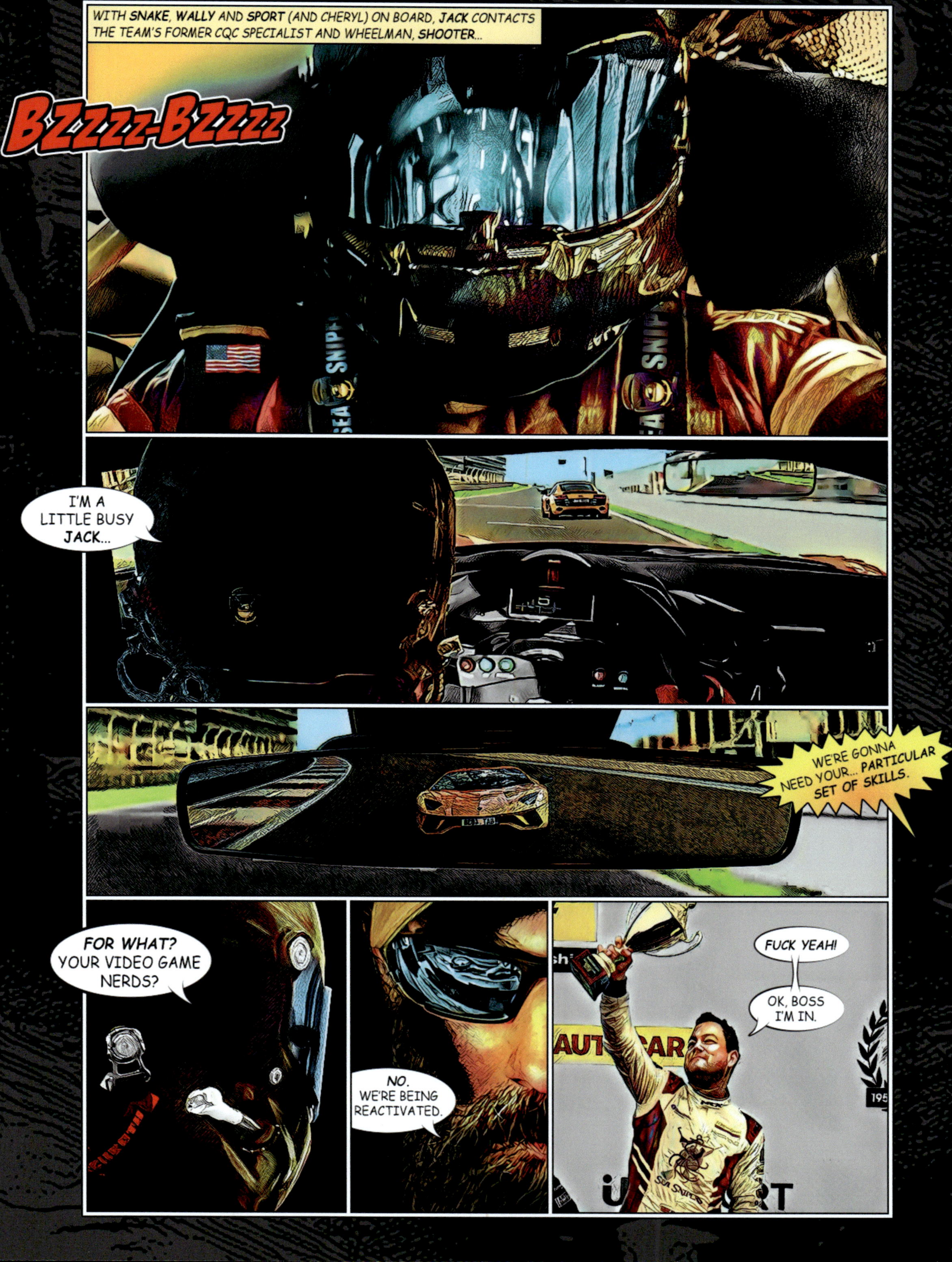
WITH SNAKE, WALLY AND SPORT (AND CHERYL) ON BOARD, JACK CONTACTS THE TEAM'S FORMER CQC SPECIALIST AND WHEELMAN, SHOOTER...
BZZZZ-BZZZZ
I'M A LITTLE BUSY JACK...
WE'RE GONNA NEED YOUR... PARTICULAR SET OF SKILLS.
FOR WHAT? YOUR VIDEO GAME NERDS?
NO. WE'RE BEING REACTIVATED.
FUCK YEAH!
OK, BOSS I'M IN.

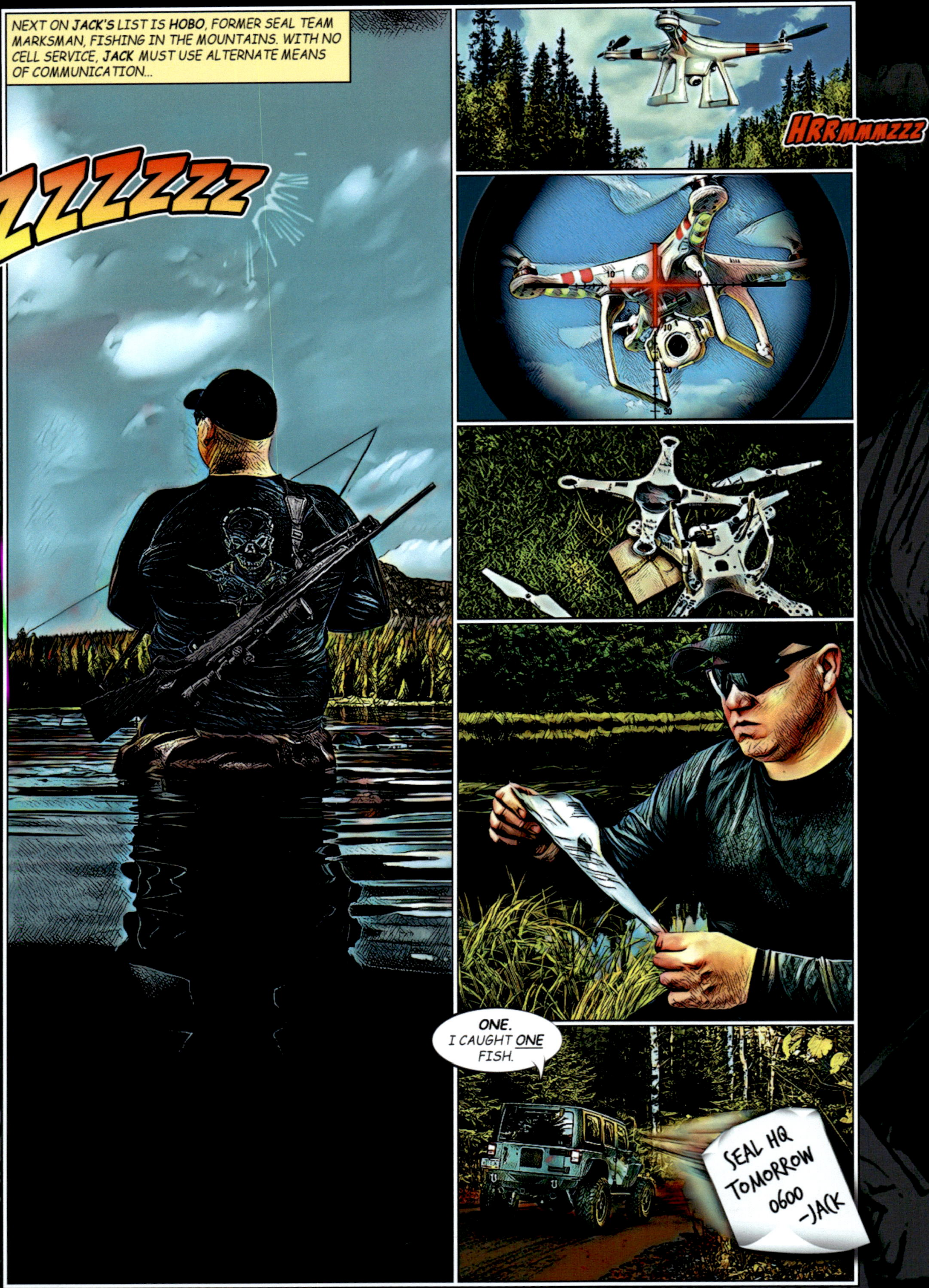

NEXT ON JACK'S LIST IS HOBO, FORMER SEAL TEAM MARKSMAN, FISHING IN THE MOUNTAINS. WITH NO CELL SERVICE, JACK MUST USE ALTERNATE MEANS OF COMMUNICATION...
ZZZZZZ
HRRMMMZZZ
ONE. I CAUGHT ONE FISH.
SEAL HQ TOMORROW 0600 -JACK

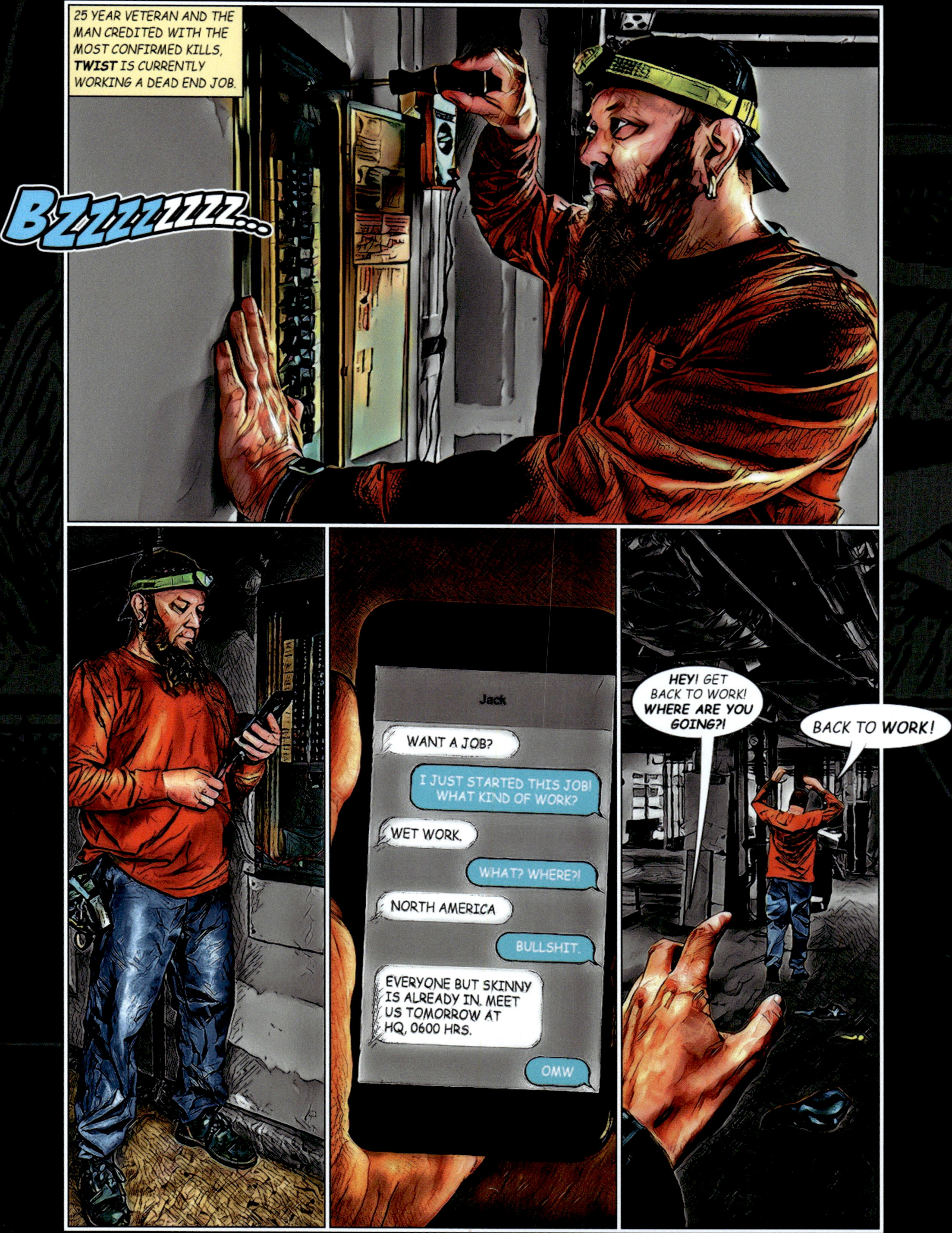
25 YEAR VETERAN AND THE MAN CREDITED WITH THE MOST CONFIRMED KILLS, **TWIST** IS CURRENTLY WORKING A DEAD END JOB.
BZZZZZZZZ...
Jack
WANT A JOB?
I JUST STARTED THIS JOB! WHAT KIND OF WORK?
WET WORK.
WHAT? WHERE?!
NORTH AMERICA
BULLSHIT.
EVERYONE BUT SKINNY IS ALREADY IN. MEET US TOMORROW AT HQ, 0600 HRS.
OMW
HEY! GET BACK TO WORK! WHERE ARE YOU GOING?!
BACK TO WORK!

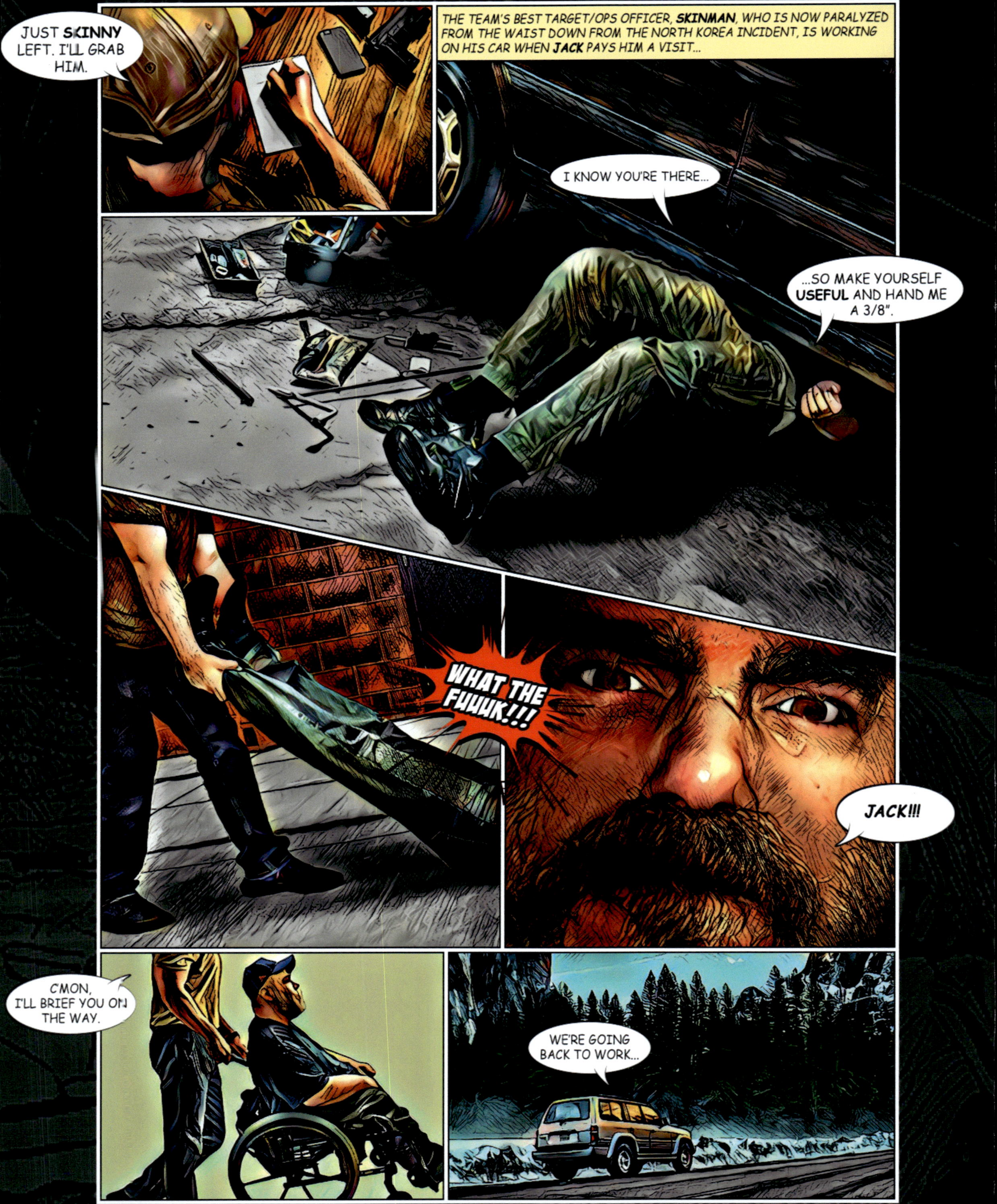
JUST SKINNY LEFT. I'LL GRAB HIM.
THE TEAM'S BEST TARGET/OPS OFFICER, SKINMAN, WHO IS NOW PARALYZED FROM THE WAIST DOWN FROM THE NORTH KOREA INCIDENT, IS WORKING ON HIS CAR WHEN JACK PAYS HIM A VISIT...
I KNOW YOU'RE THERE...
...SO MAKE YOURSELF USEFUL AND HAND ME A 3/8".
WHAT THE FUUUK!!!
JACK!!!
C'MON, I'LL BRIEF YOU ON THE WAY.
WE'RE GOING BACK TO WORK...

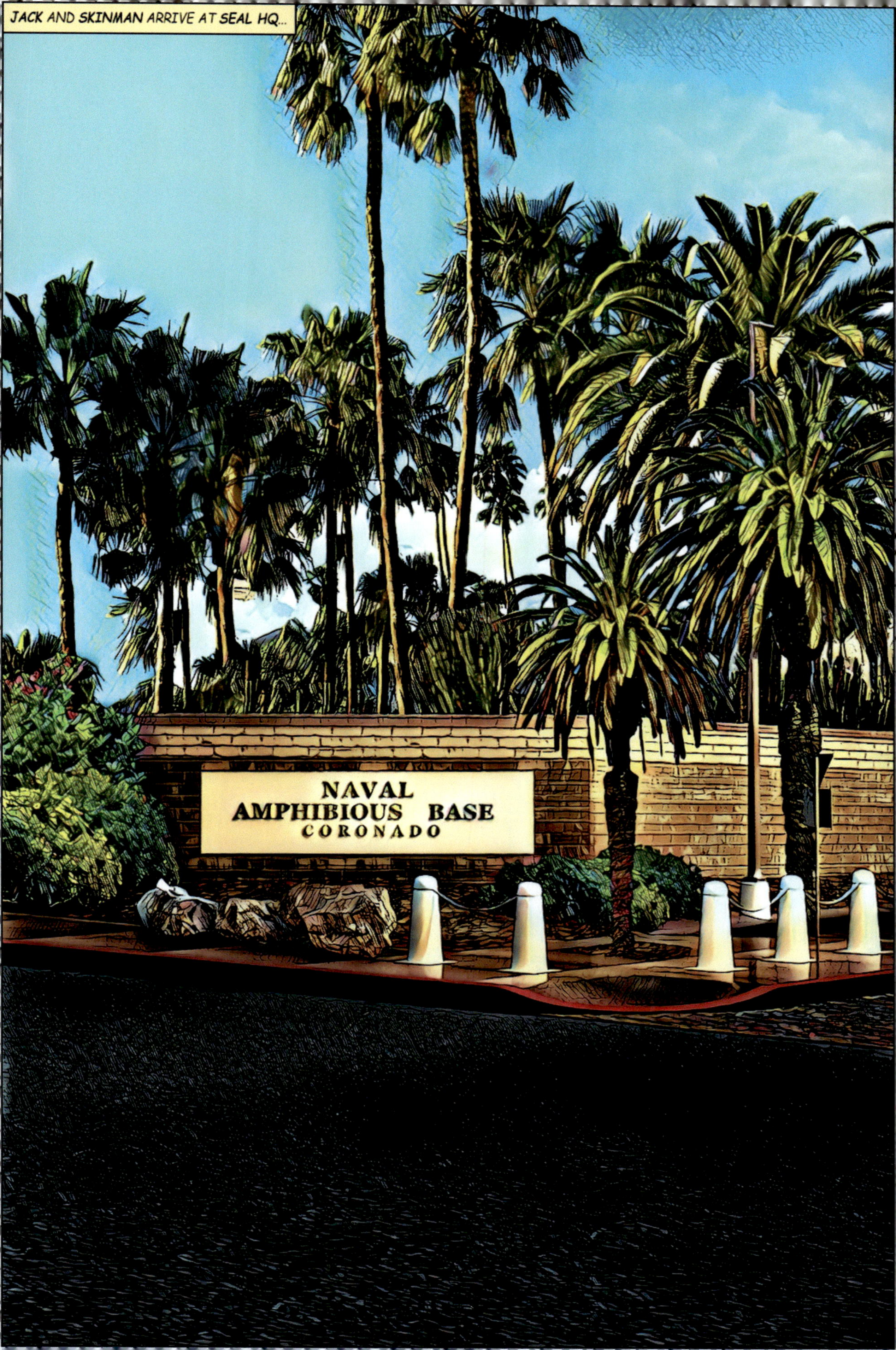
JACK AND SKINMAN ARRIVE AT SEAL HQ...
NAVAL
AMPHIBIOUS BASE
CORONADO

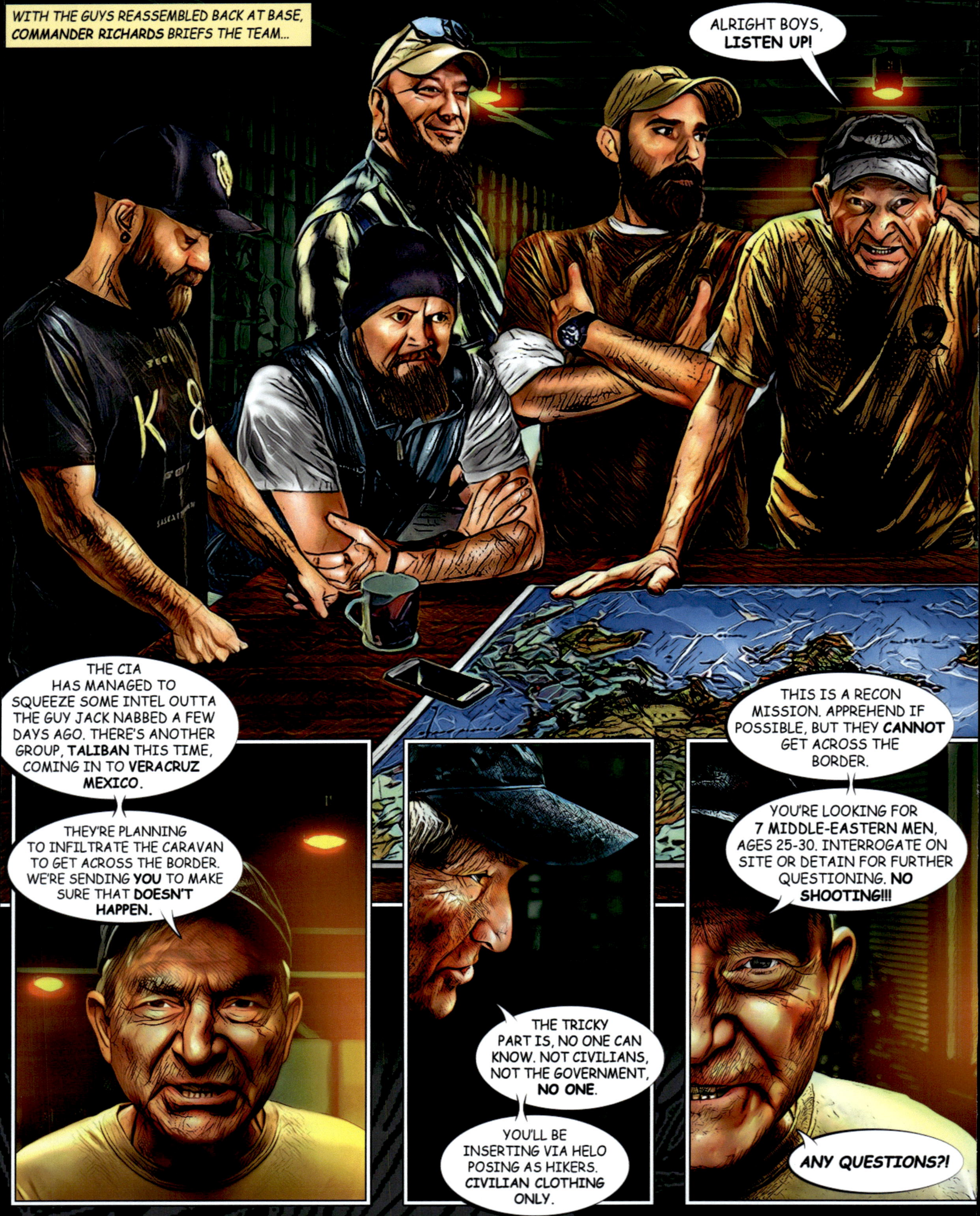
WITH THE GUYS REASSEMBLED BACK AT BASE, COMMANDER RICHARDS BRIEFS THE TEAM...
ALRIGHT BOYS, LISTEN UP!
THE CIA HAS MANAGED TO SQUEEZE SOME INTEL OUTTA THE GUY JACK NABBED A FEW DAYS AGO. THERE'S ANOTHER GROUP, TALIBAN THIS TIME, COMING IN TO VERACRUZ MEXICO.
THEY'RE PLANNING TO INFILTRATE THE CARAVAN TO GET ACROSS THE BORDER. WE'RE SENDING YOU TO MAKE SURE THAT DOESN'T HAPPEN.
THE TRICKY PART IS, NO ONE CAN KNOW. NOT CIVILIANS, NOT THE GOVERNMENT, NO ONE.
YOU'LL BE INSERTING VIA HELO POSING AS HIKERS. CIVILIAN CLOTHING ONLY.
THIS IS A RECON MISSION. APPREHEND IF POSSIBLE, BUT THEY CANNOT GET ACROSS THE BORDER.
YOU'RE LOOKING FOR 7 MIDDLE-EASTERN MEN, AGES 25-30. INTERROGATE ON SITE OR DETAIN FOR FURTHER QUESTIONING. NO SHOOTING!!!
ANY QUESTIONS?!

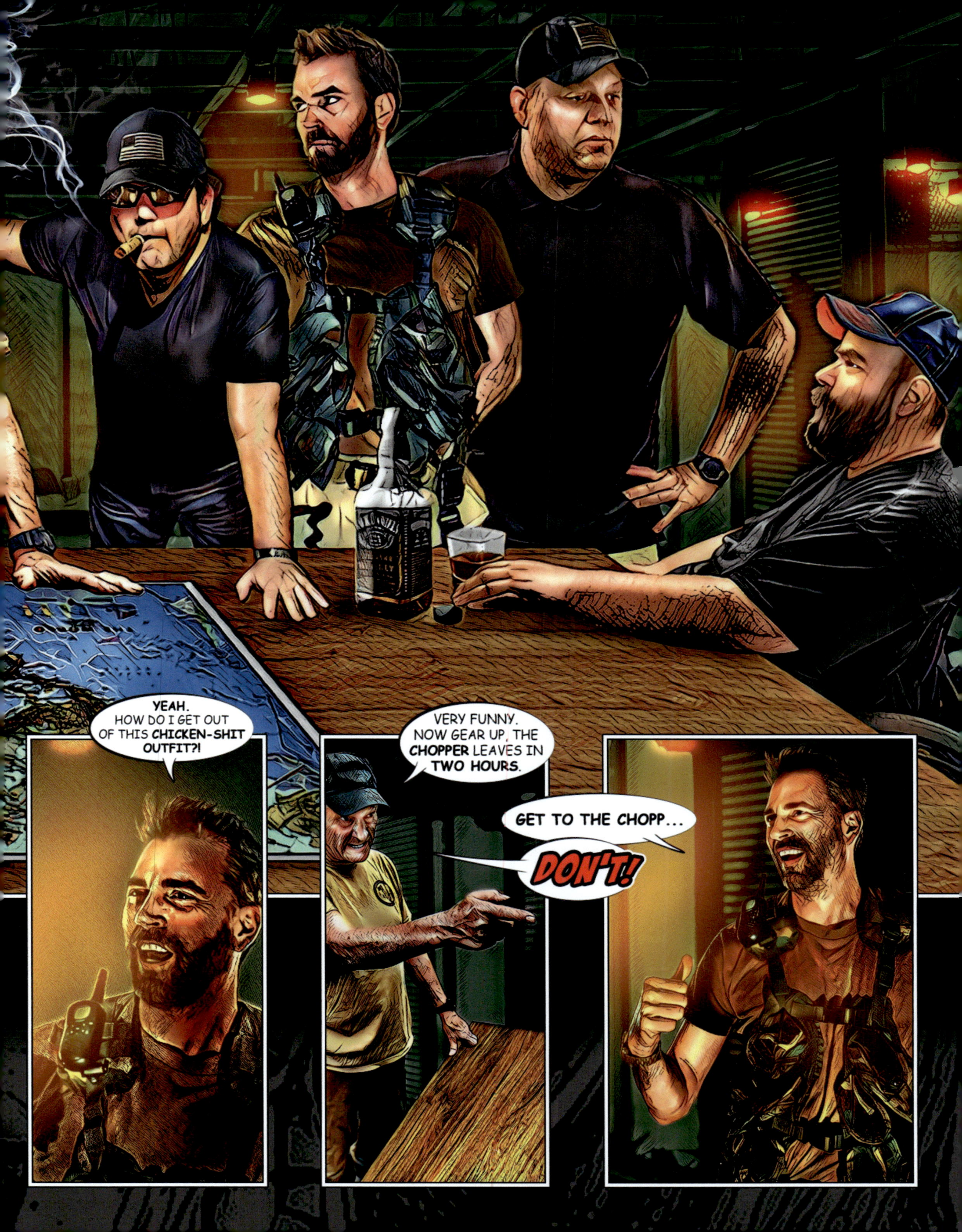
YEAH.
HOW DO I GET OUT OF THIS **CHICKEN-SHIT OUTFIT?!**
VERY FUNNY. NOW GEAR UP, THE **CHOPPER** LEAVES IN **TWO HOURS**.
GET TO THE CHOPP...
DON'T!

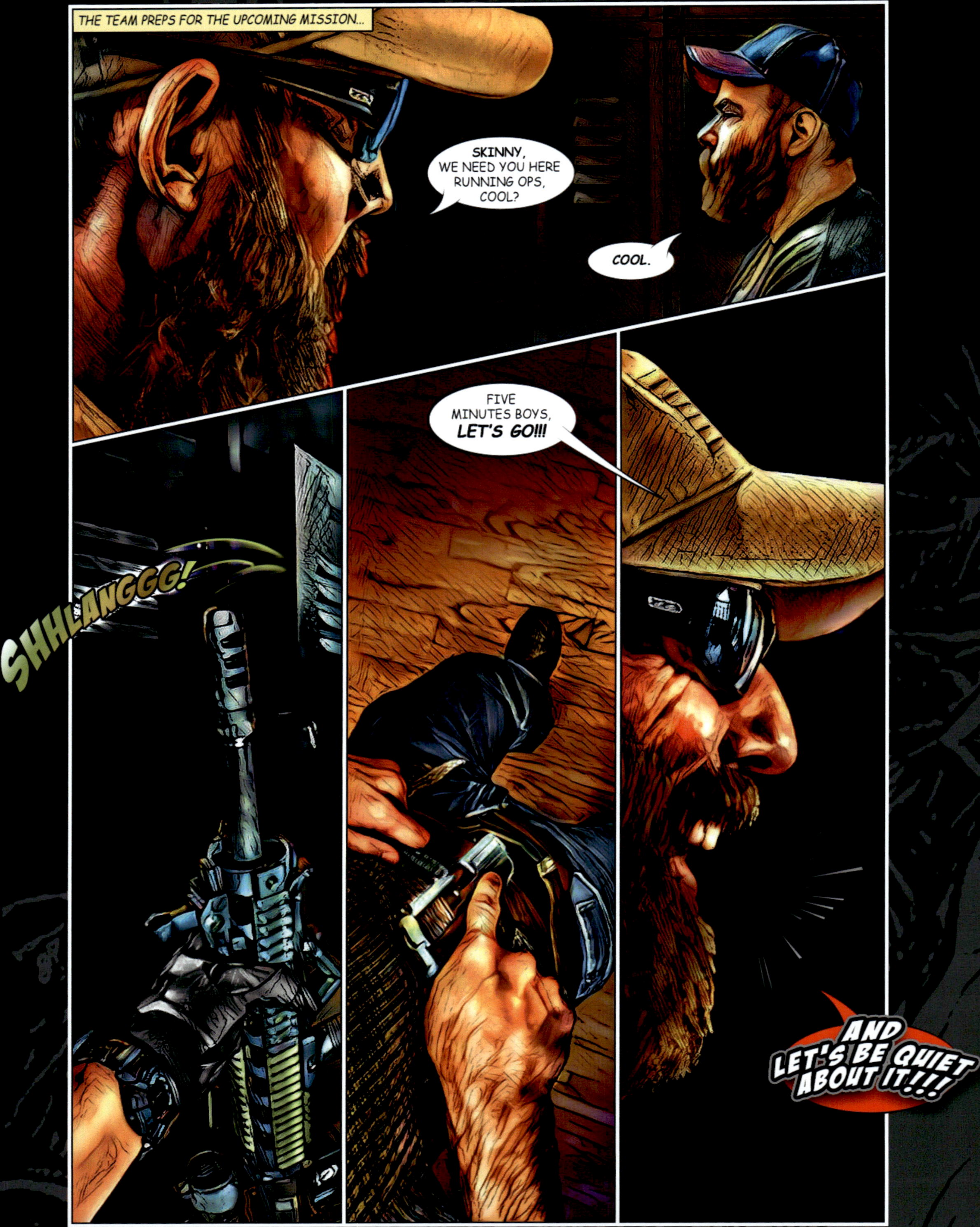
THE TEAM PREPS FOR THE UPCOMING MISSION...
SKINNY, WE NEED YOU HERE RUNNING OPS, COOL?
COOL.
SHHLANGGG!
FIVE MINUTES BOYS, LET'S GO!!!
AND LET'S BE QUIET ABOUT IT!!!

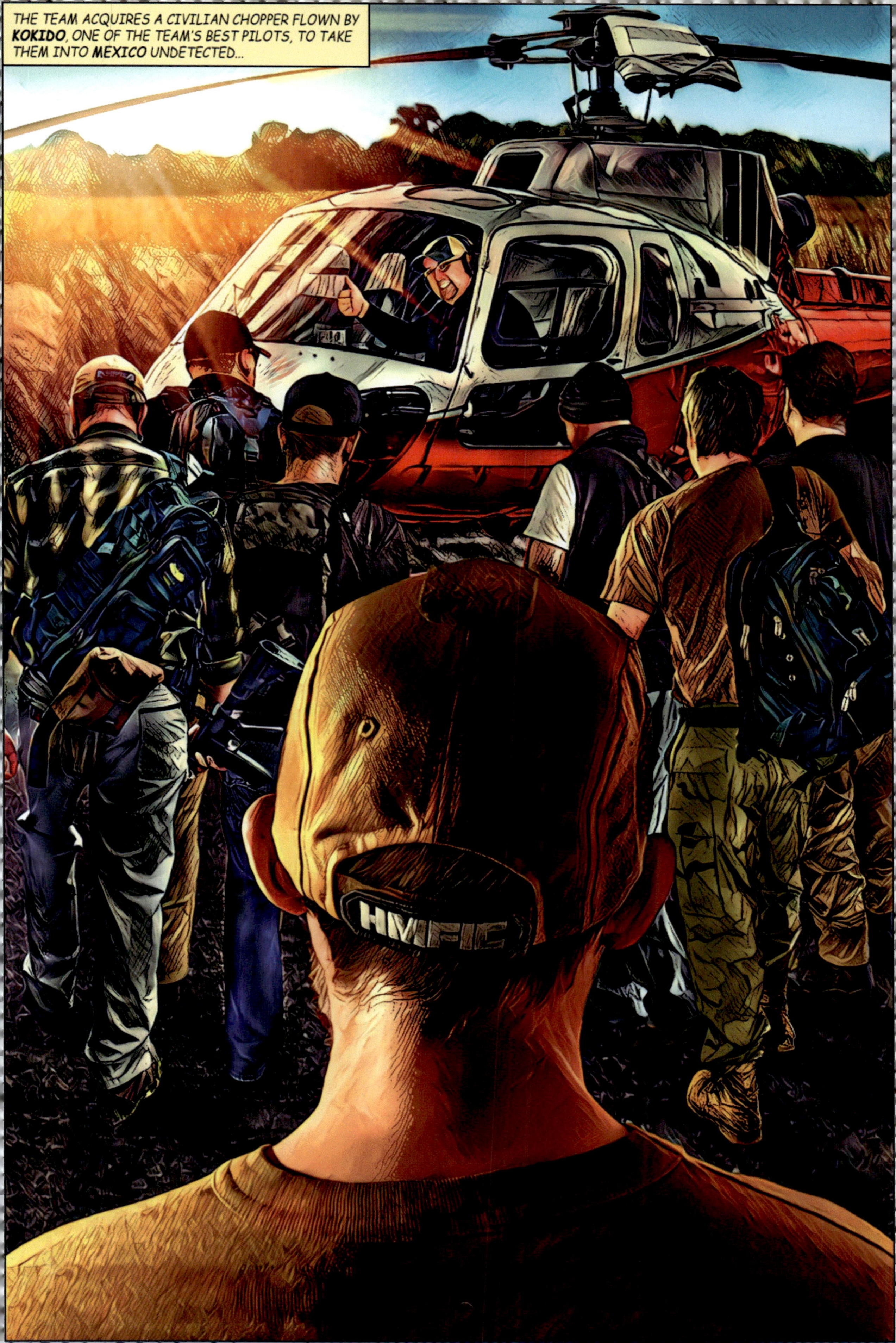
THE TEAM ACQUIRES A CIVILIAN CHOPPER FLOWN BY **KOKIDO**, ONE OF THE TEAM'S BEST PILOTS, TO TAKE THEM INTO **MEXICO** UNDETECTED...
HMFIC

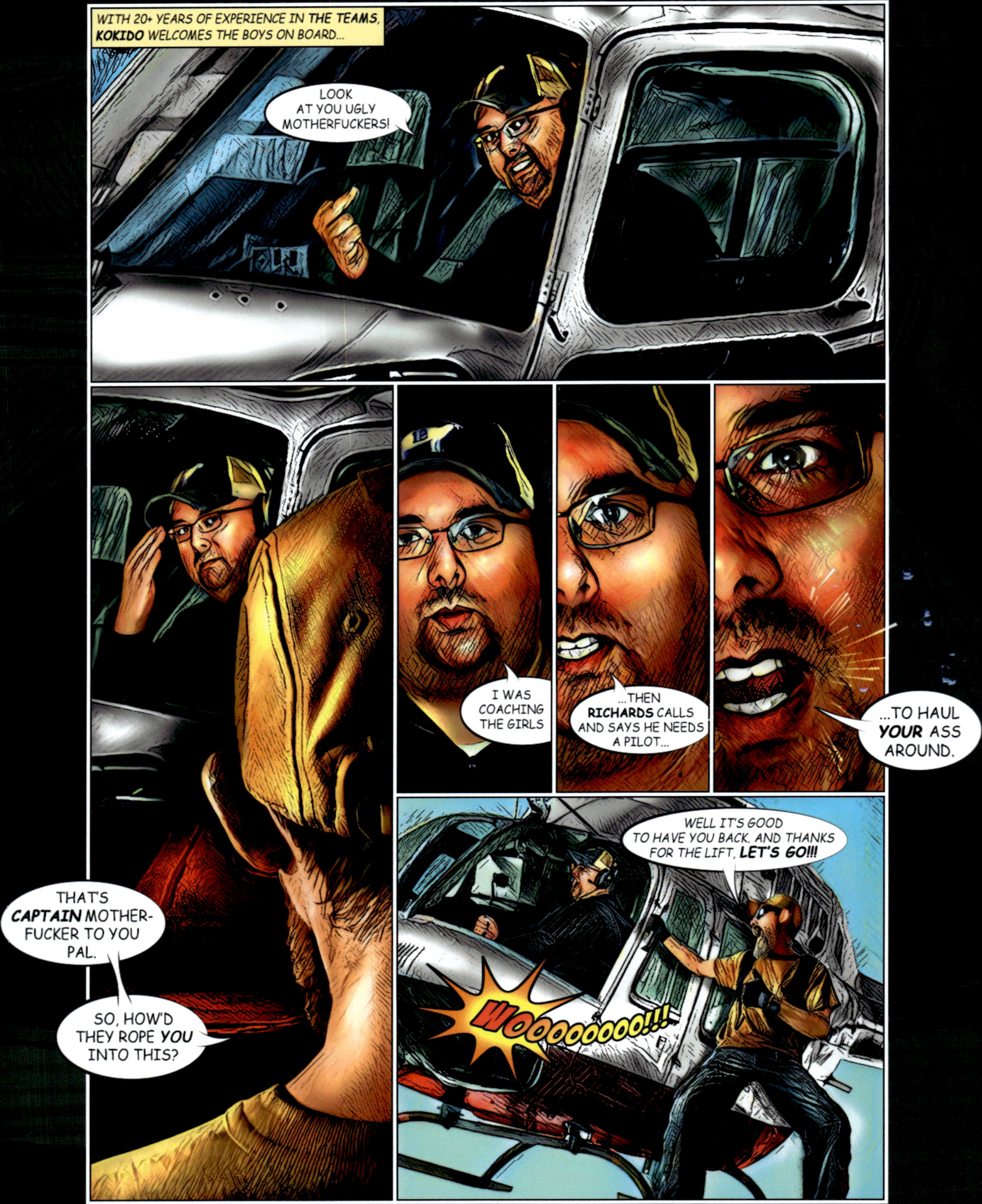
WITH 20+ YEARS OF EXPERIENCE IN THE TEAMS, KOKIDO WELCOMES THE BOYS ON BOARD...
LOOK AT YOU UGLY MOTHERFUCKERS!
THAT'S CAPTAIN MOTHER-FUCKER TO YOU PAL.
SO, HOW'D THEY ROPE YOU INTO THIS?
I WAS COACHING THE GIRLS
...THEN RICHARDS CALLS AND SAYS HE NEEDS A PILOT...
...TO HAUL YOUR ASS AROUND.
WELL IT'S GOOD TO HAVE YOU BACK. AND THANKS FOR THE LIFT, LET'S GO!!!
WOOOOOOOO!!!

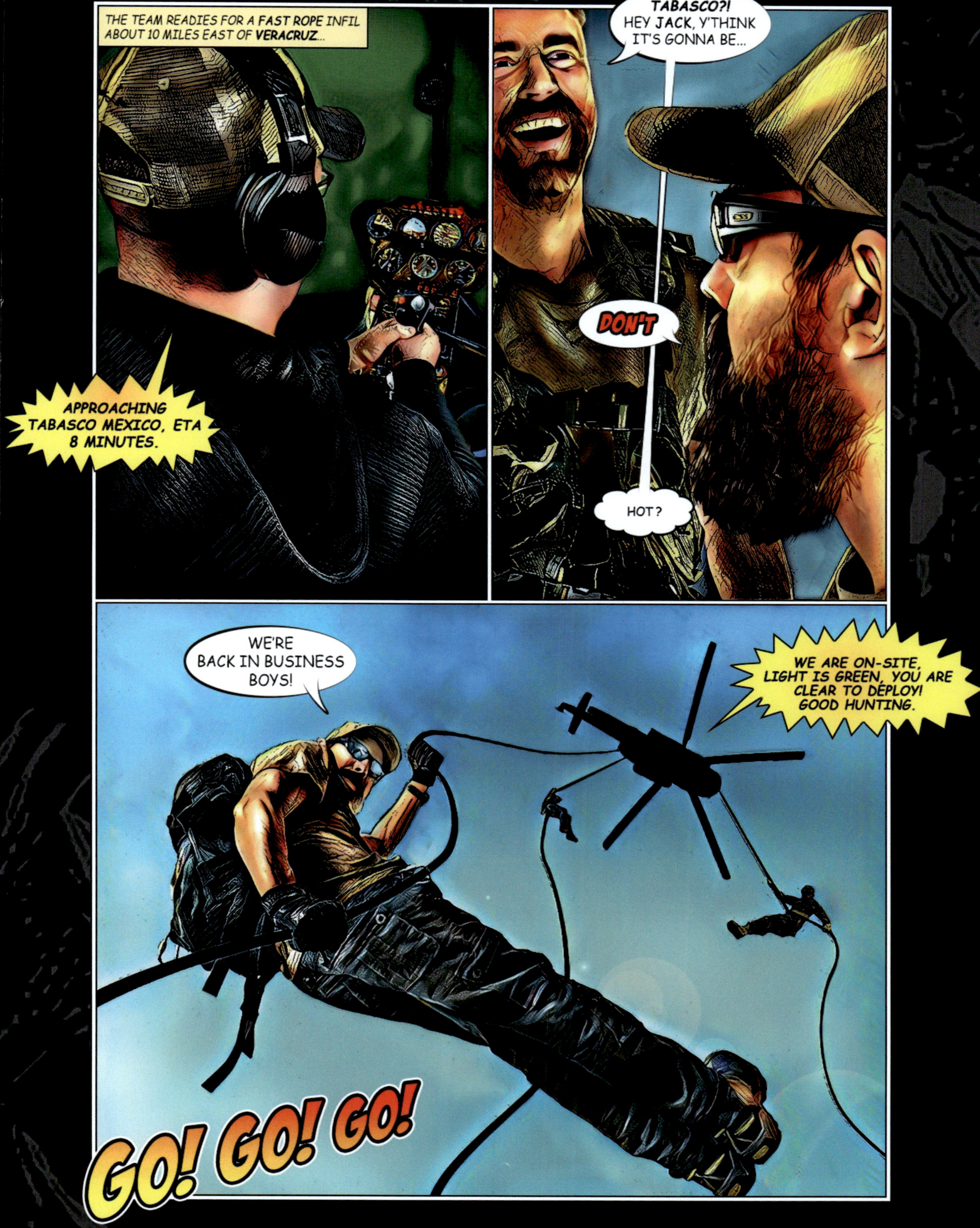
THE TEAM READIES FOR A FAST ROPE INFIL ABOUT 10 MILES EAST OF VERACRUZ...
APPROACHING TABASCO MEXICO, ETA 8 MINUTES.
TABASCO?! HEY JACK, Y'THINK IT'S GONNA BE...
DON'T
HOT?
WE'RE BACK IN BUSINESS BOYS!
WE ARE ON-SITE, LIGHT IS GREEN, YOU ARE CLEAR TO DEPLOY! GOOD HUNTING.
GO! GO! GO!

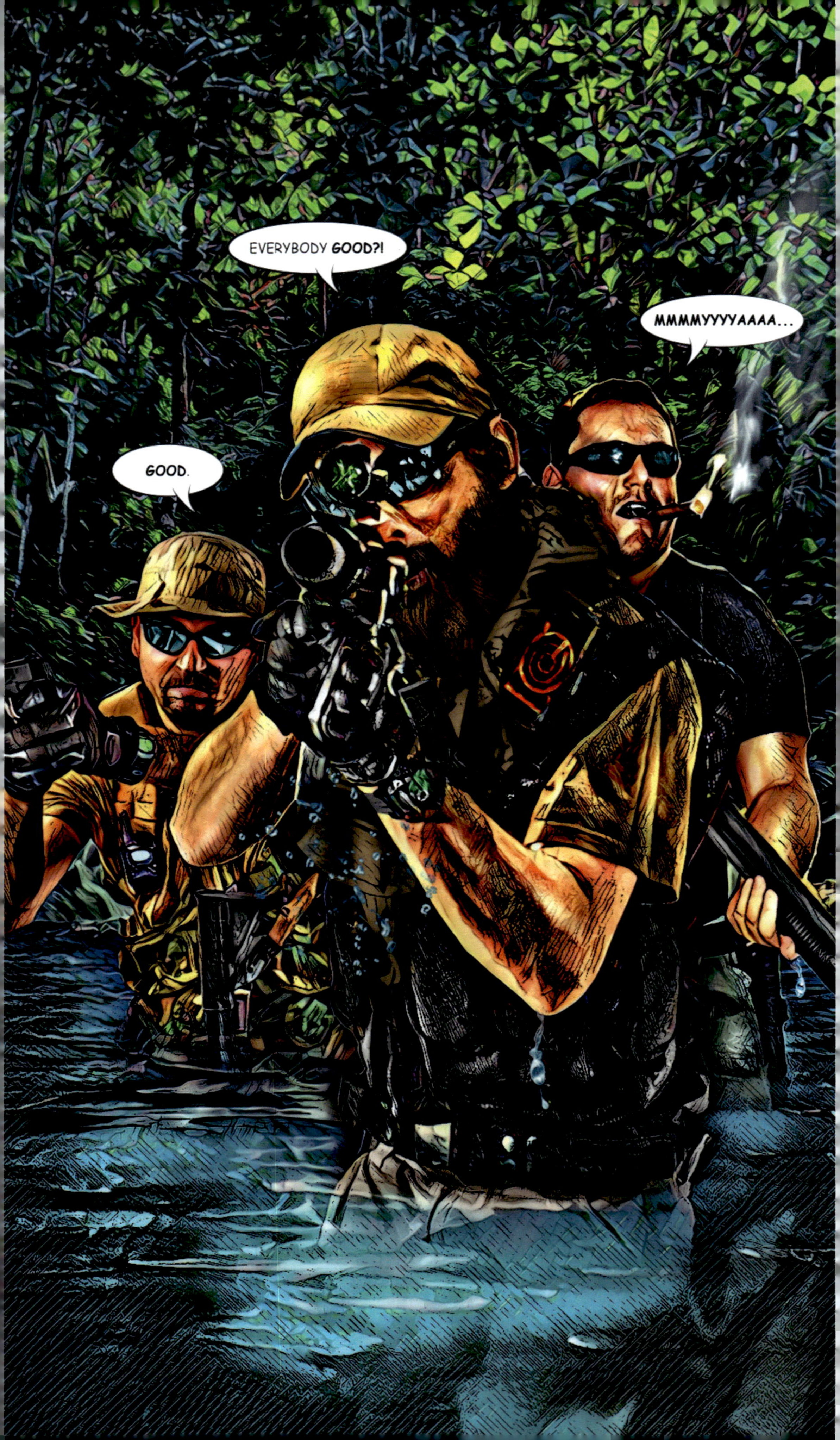
EVERYBODY GOOD?!
GOOD.
MMMMYYYYAAAA...

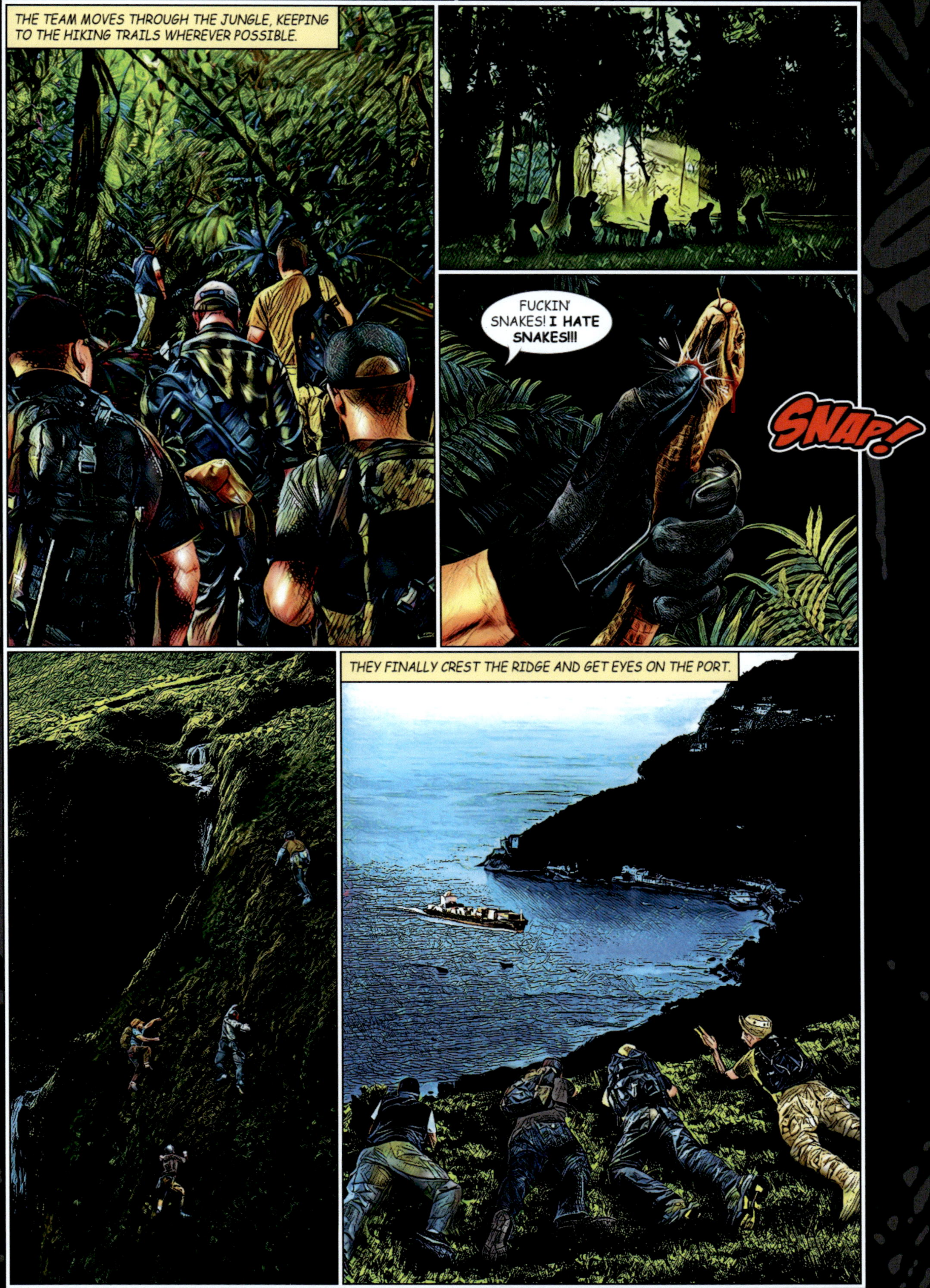
THE TEAM MOVES THROUGH THE JUNGLE, KEEPING TO THE HIKING TRAILS WHEREVER POSSIBLE.
FUCKIN' SNAKES! I HATE SNAKES!!!
SNAP!
THEY FINALLY CREST THE RIDGE AND GET EYES ON THE PORT.

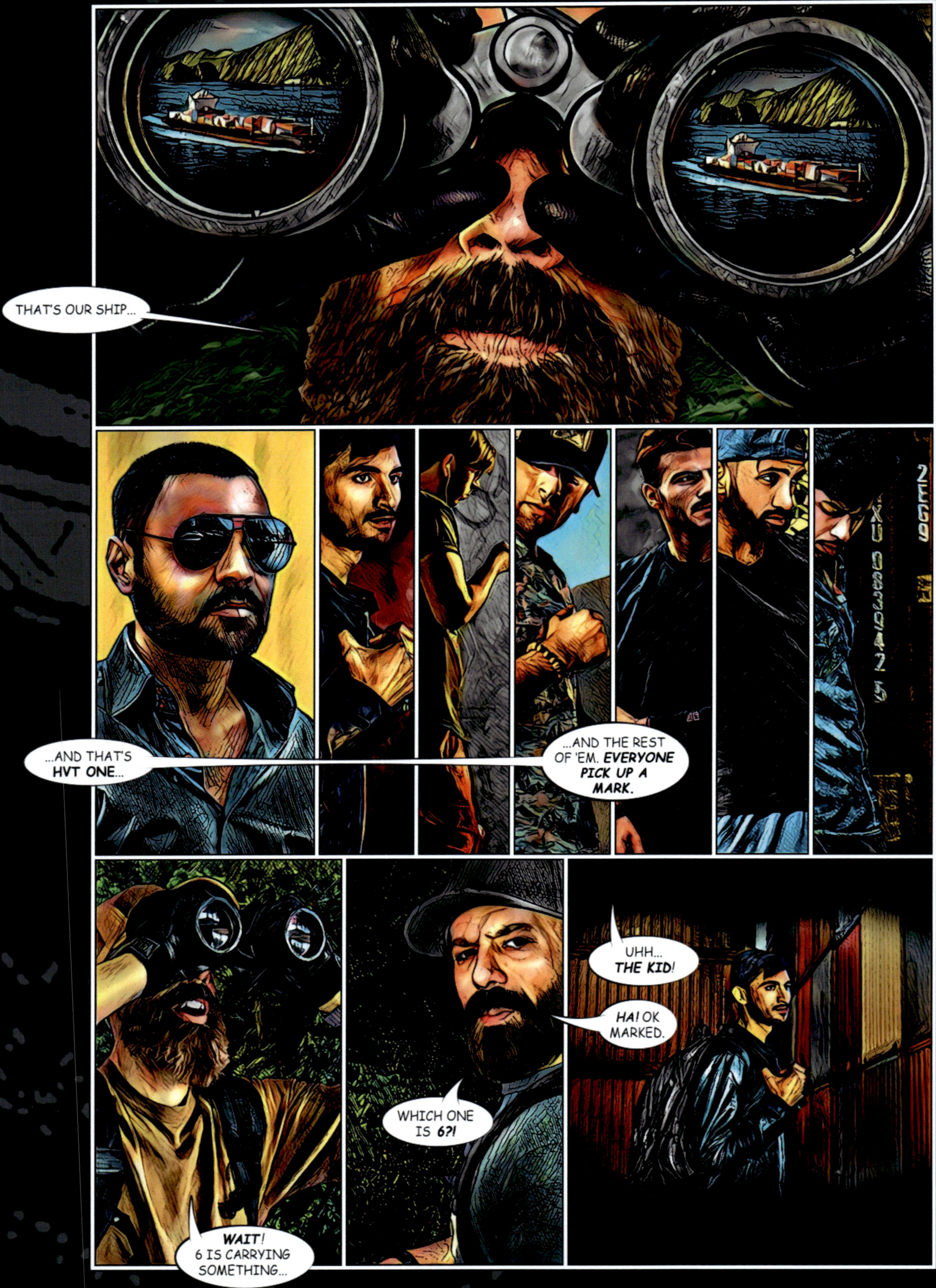
THAT'S OUR SHIP...
...AND THAT'S HVT ONE...
...AND THE REST OF 'EM. EVERYONE PICK UP A MARK.
WAIT! 6 IS CARRYING SOMETHING...
WHICH ONE IS 6?!
HA! OK MARKED.
UHH... THE KID!

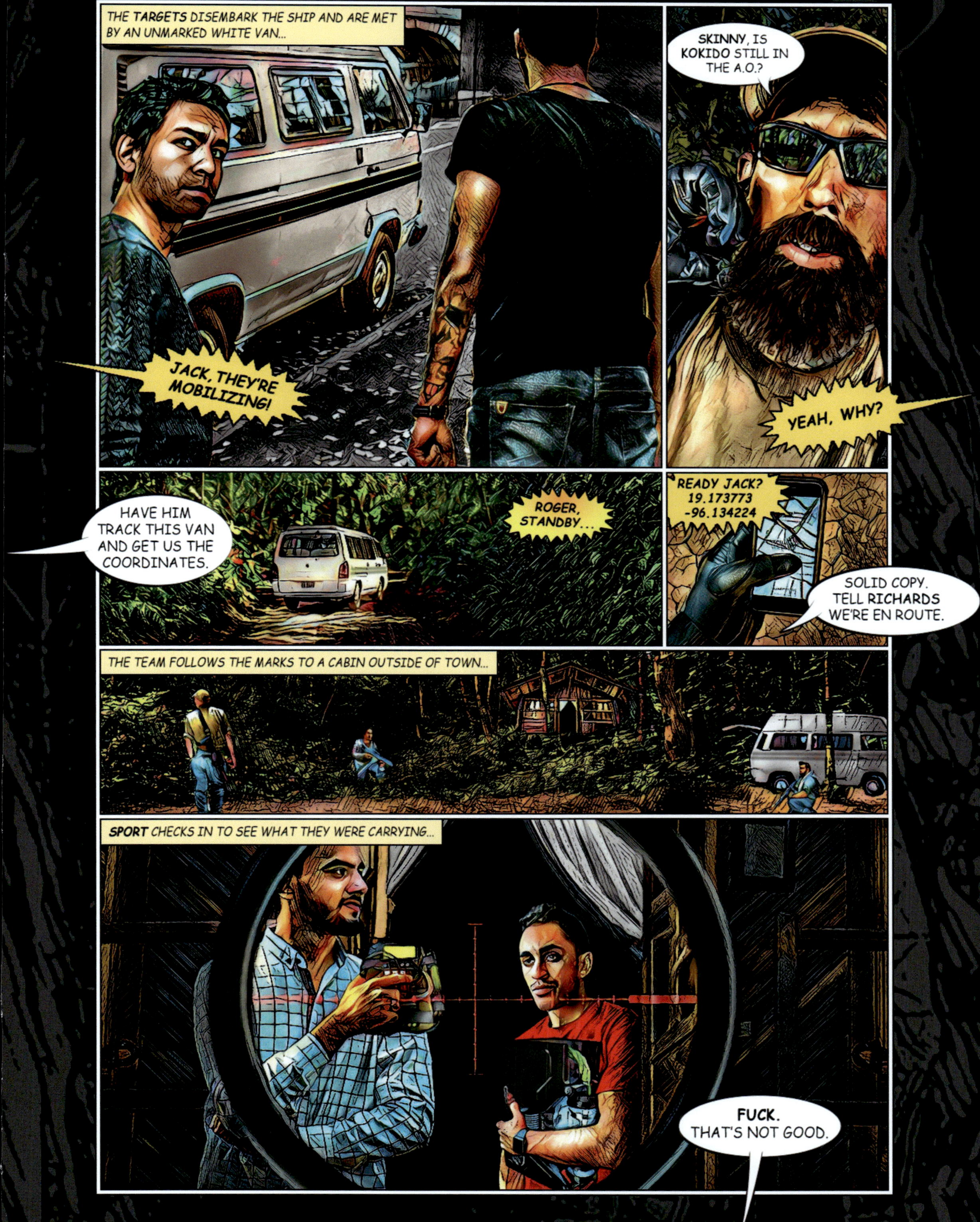
THE TARGETS DISEMBARK THE SHIP AND ARE MET BY AN UNMARKED WHITE VAN...
JACK, THEY'RE MOBILIZING!
SKINNY, IS KOKIDO STILL IN THE A.O.?
YEAH, WHY?
HAVE HIM TRACK THIS VAN AND GET US THE COORDINATES.
ROGER, STANDBY...
READY JACK? 19.173773 -96.134224
SOLID COPY. TELL RICHARDS WE'RE EN ROUTE.
THE TEAM FOLLOWS THE MARKS TO A CABIN OUTSIDE OF TOWN...
SPORT CHECKS IN TO SEE WHAT THEY WERE CARRYING...
FUCK. THAT'S NOT GOOD.

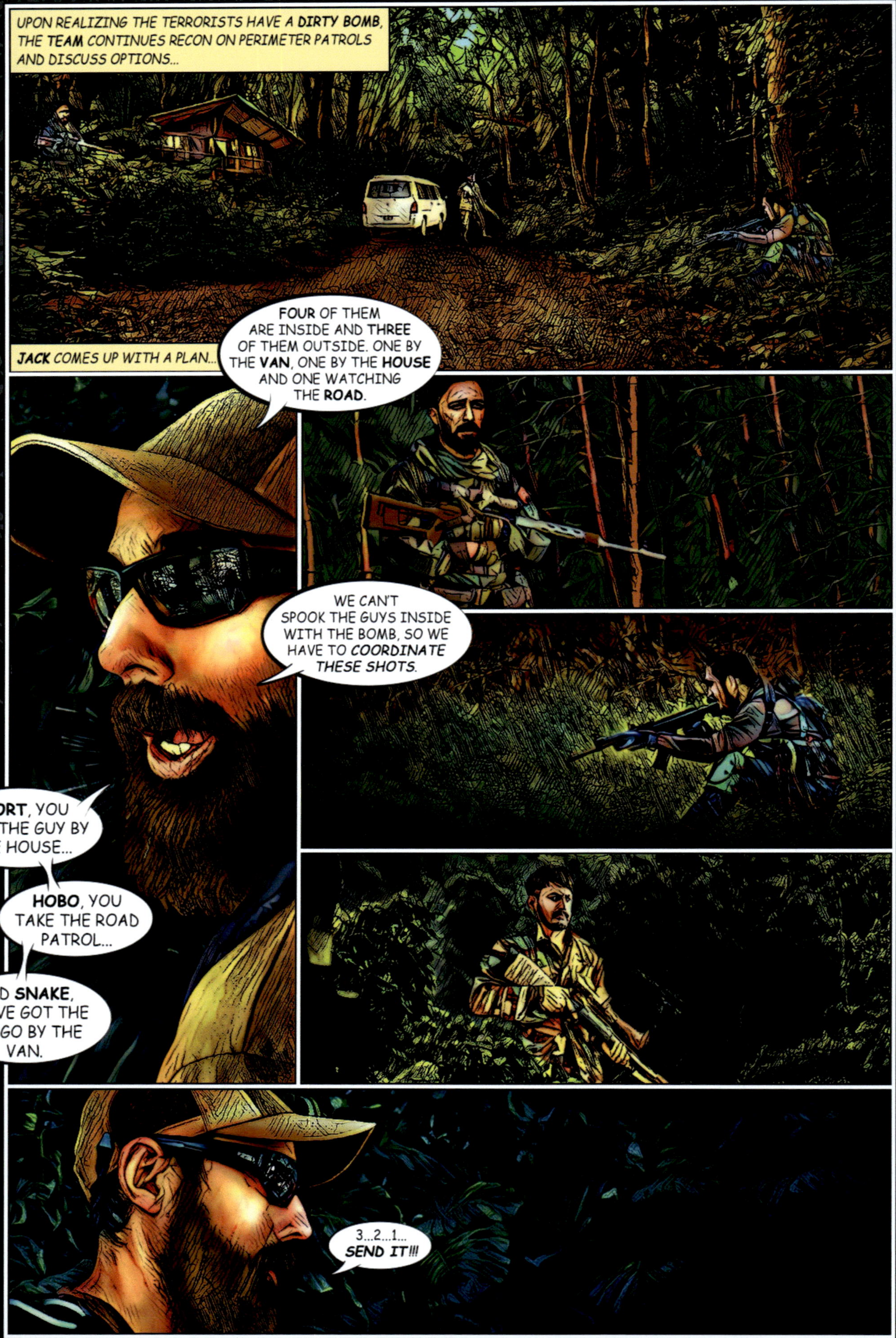

UPON REALIZING THE TERRORISTS HAVE A DIRTY BOMB, THE TEAM CONTINUES RECON ON PERIMETER PATROLS AND DISCUSS OPTIONS...
JACK COMES UP WITH A PLAN...
FOUR OF THEM ARE INSIDE AND THREE OF THEM OUTSIDE. ONE BY THE VAN, ONE BY THE HOUSE AND ONE WATCHING THE ROAD.
WE CAN'T SPOOK THE GUYS INSIDE WITH THE BOMB, SO WE HAVE TO COORDINATE THESE SHOTS.
SPORT, YOU TAKE THE GUY BY THE HOUSE...
HOBO, YOU TAKE THE ROAD PATROL...
AND SNAKE, YOU'VE GOT THE TANGO BY THE VAN.
3...2...1... SEND IT!!!

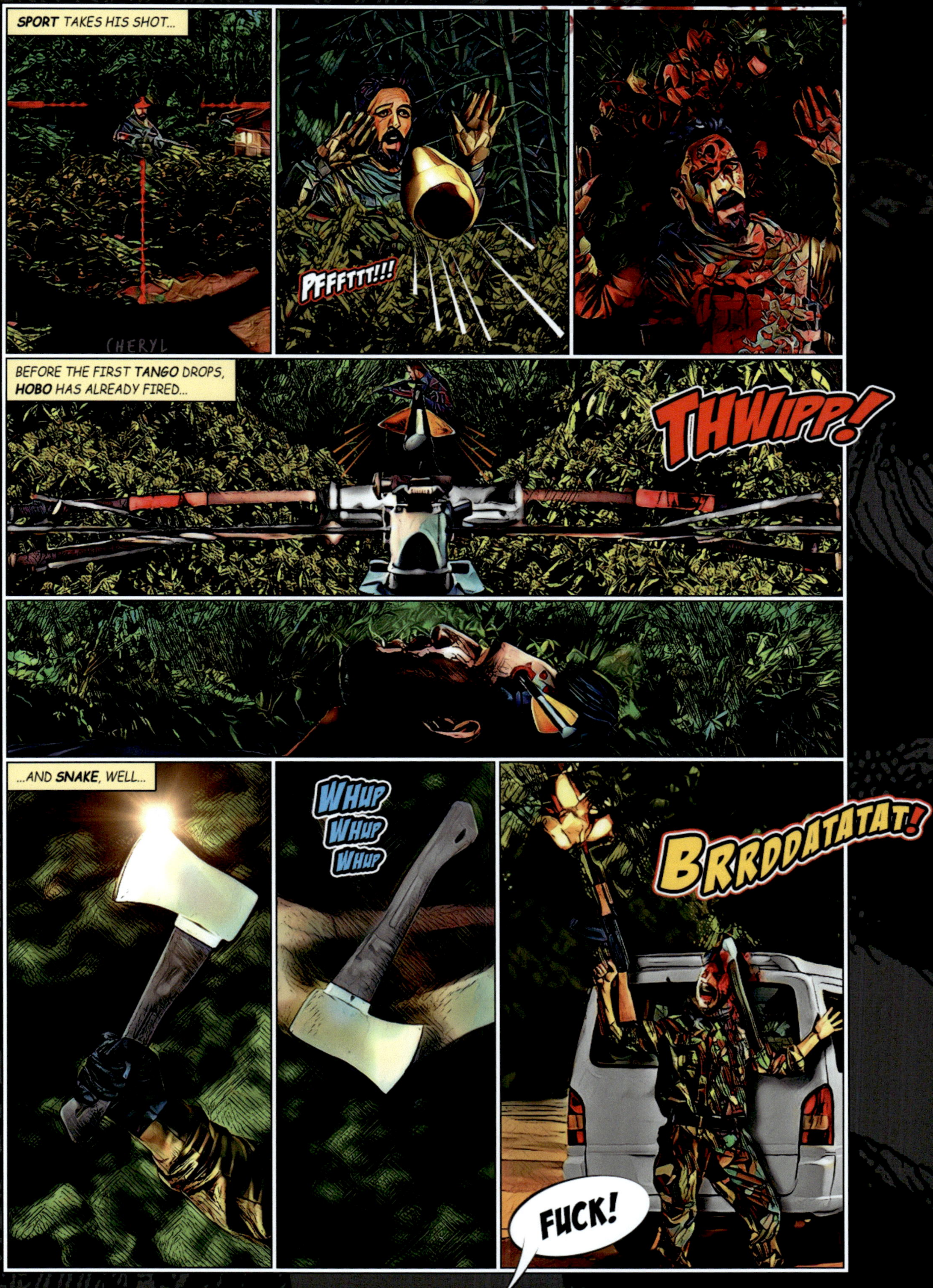

SPORT TAKES HIS SHOT...
CHERYL
PFFFTTT!!!
BEFORE THE FIRST TANGO DROPS, HOBO HAS ALREADY FIRED...
THWIPP!
...AND SNAKE, WELL...
WHUP
WHUP
WHUP
BRRDDATATAT!
FUCK!

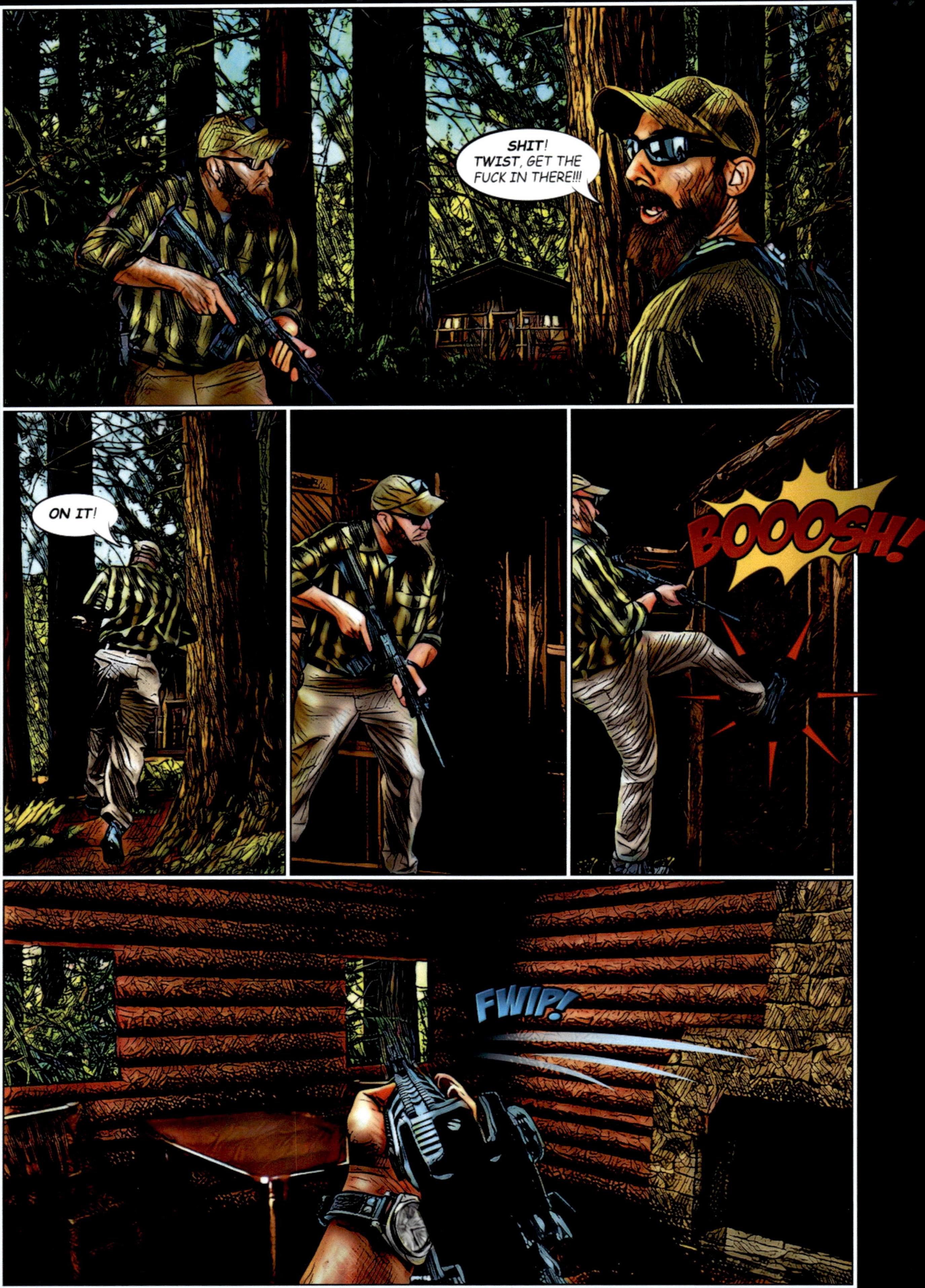
SHIT! TWIST, GET THE FUCK IN THERE!!!
ON IT!
BOOOSH!
FWIP!

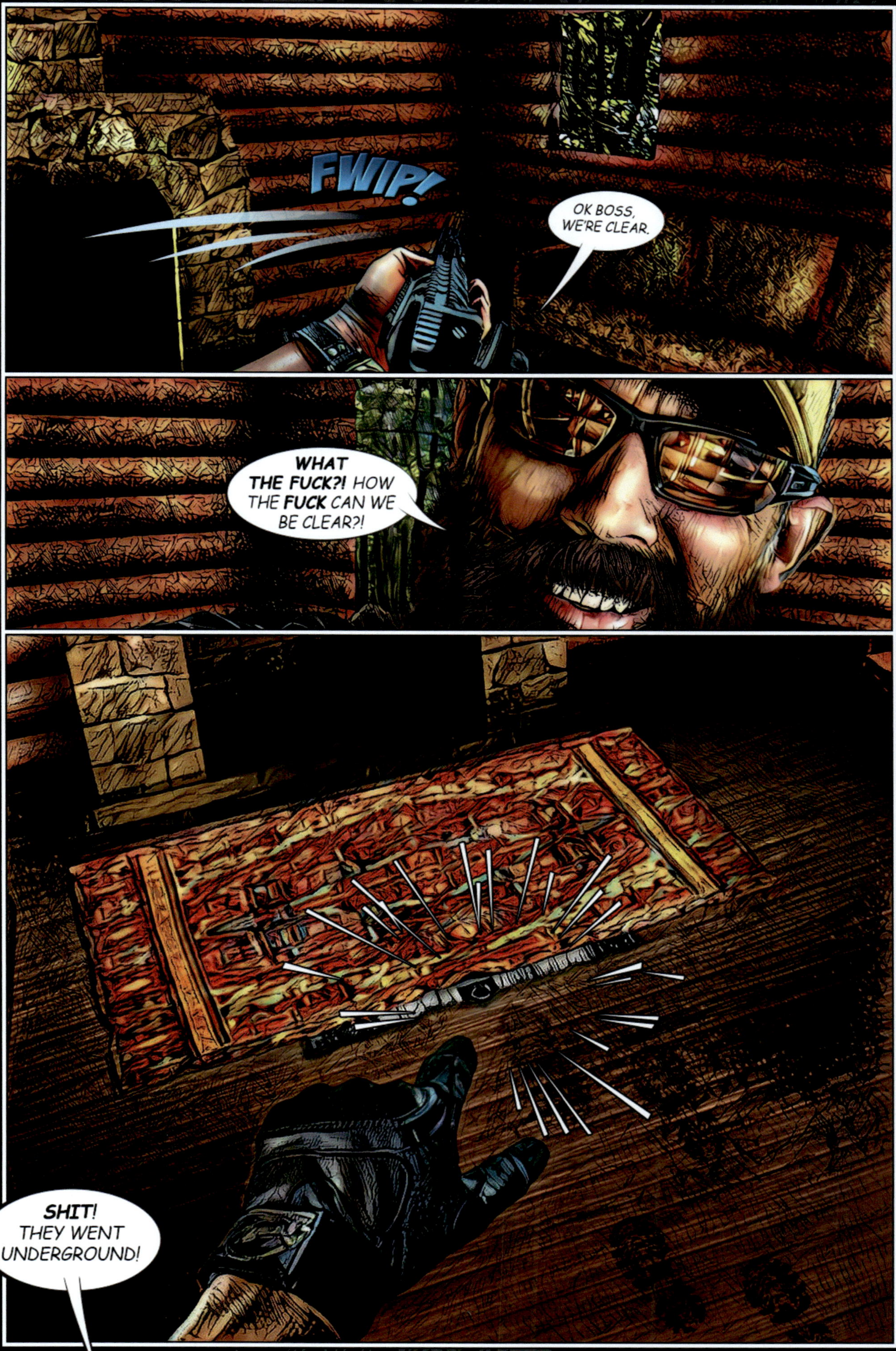
FWIP!
OK BOSS, WE'RE CLEAR.
WHAT THE FUCK?! HOW THE FUCK CAN WE BE CLEAR?!
SHIT! THEY WENT UNDERGROUND!

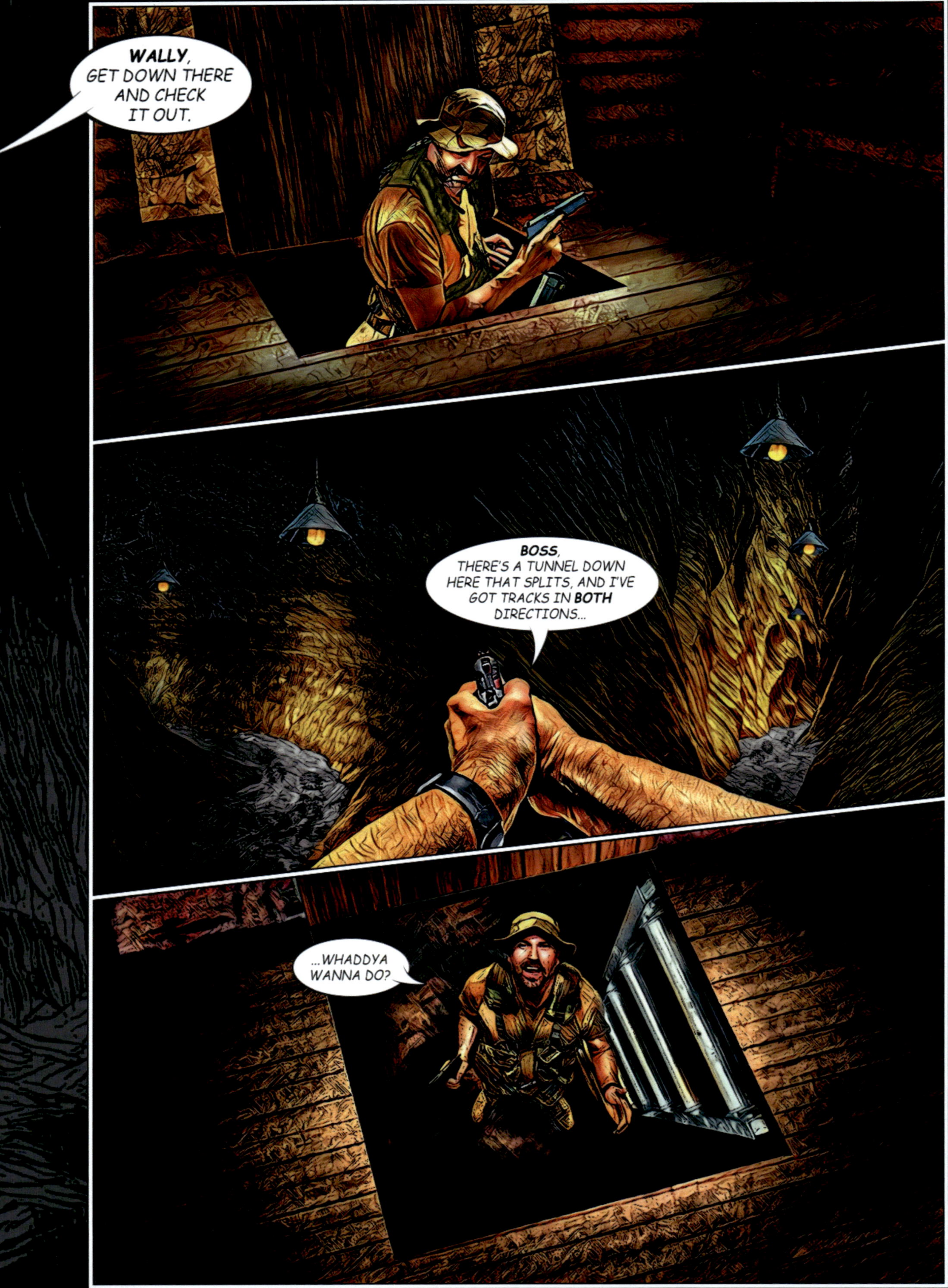
WALLY, GET DOWN THERE AND CHECK IT OUT.
BOSS, THERE'S A TUNNEL DOWN HERE THAT SPLITS, AND I'VE GOT TRACKS IN **BOTH** DIRECTIONS...
...WHADDYA WANNA DO?

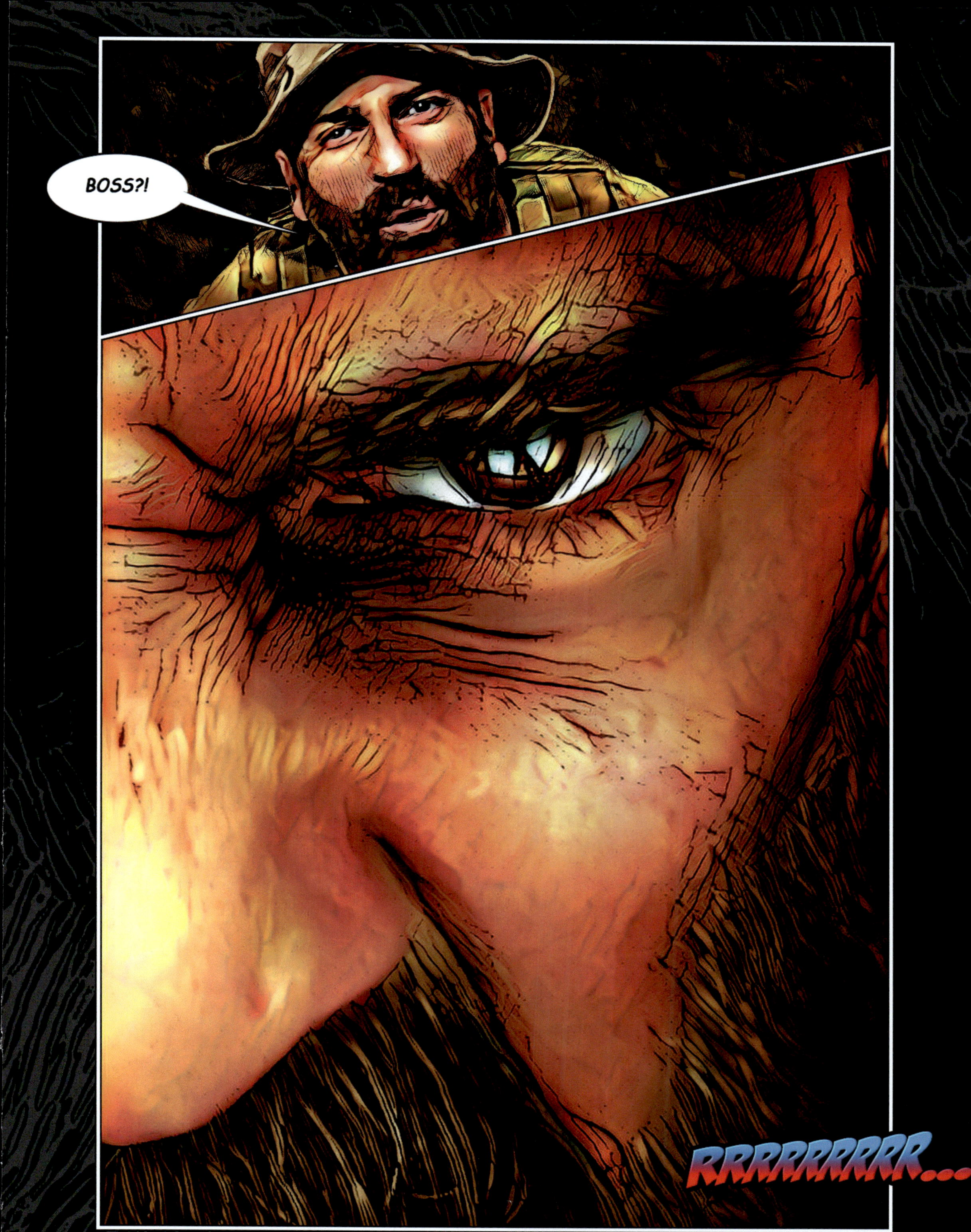
BOSS?!
RRRRRRRRR...

THIS BOOK IS DEDICATED TO PHILLIP PERRY — A SEA SNIPER OPERATOR FOR EIGHT YEARS

SKINMAN

VALHALLA 1973 – 2021 · JOINED 2013 – FOREVER

YOU CAME LOOKING TO BELONG
WE SAID THERE WAS NO SPACE
YOU BIDED YOUR TIME
'TIL WE FOUND YOU A PLACE

WITHOUT COMPLAINTS YOU LEARNED
TO BE A SOLDIER FROM THE START
WE NEVER TREATED YOU DIFFERENTLY
YOU COMMITTED YOUR HEART

YOU GAVE YOURSELF TO THE TEAM
BATTLED THROUGH SICKNESS
THEN YOU WERE TAKEN
AND WE HAD TO WITNESS

WITH HONOR AND VALOR
YOU FOUGHT EACH NIGHT
OUR BROTHER IN ARMS
STILL HAS AN INVITE

WE MISS YOU SKINNY. FAIR WINDS AND FOLLOWING SEAS